DA

'If I kissed you now, you'd kiss me right back.'

The truth felt like a blast of cold air. Flora took a deep breath. Why was she fighting it? Would it really matter if she took Massimo's hand and led him to some anonymous hotel in the town? For a moment she could almost feel the weight of the door key in her hand. Could feel the shimmering heat between their naked bodies. Only…

She straightened her shoulders. Sex made everything *seem* so simple. All it required was some bodies and the right mix of hormones. But, no matter how much she ached to feel the weight of his body on hers, she wasn't going to give in.

She breathed out slowly as, behind her, a bus pulled noisily into the square. 'Yes. I kissed you,' she said defiantly. 'And I'm not going to pretend that I didn't enjoy it, or that I don't find you attractive. Only it's not enough. Not enough for me to sleep with you. It might have been if we felt the same way. But we both know your motives have nothing to do with passion and everything to do with paying me back for getting in your way.'

Louise Fuller was a tomboy who hated pink and always wanted to be the prince—not the princess! Now she enjoys creating heroines who aren't pretty pushovers but are strong, believable women. Before writing for Mills & Boon she studied literature and philosophy at university and then worked as a reporter on her local newspaper. She lives in Tunbridge Wells with her impossibly handsome husband, Patrick, and their six children.

Books by Louise Fuller

Mills & Boon Modern Romance

Vows Made in Secret

Visit the Author Profile page at
millsandboon.co.uk.

A DEAL SEALED BY PASSION

BY
LOUISE FULLER

First published in Great Britain 2016
By Mills & Boon, an imprint of HarperCollins*Publishers*
1 London Bridge Street, London, SE1 9GF

© 2016 Louise Fuller

ISBN: 978-0-263-26359-6

Our policy is to use papers that are natural, renewable and recyclable
products and made from wood grown in sustainable forests. The logging
and manufacturing processes conform to the legal environmental
regulations of the country of origin.

Printed and bound in Great Britain
by CPI Antony Rowe, Chippenham, Wiltshire

A DEAL SEALED
BY PASSION

For my children:
Georgia, Eleanor, Hugo, Archie, Agatha and Millicent.
Thank you for letting me stay in my cupboard.
I love you all. x

CHAPTER ONE

IN THE DARKENED bedroom of his penthouse hotel suite Massimo Sforza gazed in silence at the illuminated numerals of his watch. It was almost time. He held his breath, waiting, and then there was a quiet but audible beep. He breathed out slowly. Midnight.

His lean, dark features tightening, he shifted his gaze and stared down dispassionately at the naked women sprawled over both him and one another in the emperor-sized bed. They were beautiful and wanton and idly he tried to remember their names. Not that it mattered. He would never see either of them again. Women had a tendency to confuse intimacy with commitment but he liked variety and anyway the 'c' word was simply not part of his vocabulary.

The brunette shifted in her sleep, her arms flopping onto his chest. Feeling a spasm of irritation, he reached down and lifted the tangle of limbs away from his torso and onto the rumpled sheets before rolling over and out of the bed.

His breathing quiet and measured, he stood up and began to pick his way between the shoes and stockings strewn across the soft pale grey carpet. In front of the huge panoramic window that covered the length of the apartment he noticed a half-empty bottle of champagne and, leaning over, he picked it up.

'Happy Birthday, Massimo,' he murmured and, lifting it to his lips, he tipped it up. He made a moue of disgust. Flat and sour—like his mood. Grimacing, he looked down at the street below. He hated birthdays. Particularly his own. All that faux sentiment and ersatz celebration.

A signature on a contract. Now, *that* was a reason to celebrate. He smiled grimly. Take the latest addition to his ever-expanding property portfolio: a six-storey nine-teen-thirties building in the exclusive Parioli district of Rome. He'd had his pick of five properties, two in the most sought-after road in the area: the Via dei Monti. His eyes gleamed. He could have bought them all—he still might. But the one he'd finally chosen hadn't even been for sale.

Which was why he'd had to have it.

He gave a small tight smile. The owners had refused to sell. But their refusal had simply fuelled his determination to win. And he always won in the end. His smile widened. Which reminded him: those glitches in the Sardinian project should finally have been ironed out. He frowned. And about time too. Patience might be a virtue but he'd waited long enough.

Behind him, one of the women moaned softly, and he felt a frisson of lust shudder over his skin. Besides, right now, he was more interested in vice than virtue.

Savouring his body's growing arousal, he glanced at the sky. It was nearly dawn. The project meeting was scheduled for that morning. He hadn't been planning to attend—but what better birthday present could there be than hearing first-hand that the last remaining obstacle had been removed? And that work on his largest and most prestigious resort ever could finally begin.

His eyes narrowed as the blonde lifted her head, her lips curving into a suggestive pout. Coolly, he smiled back at her. Perhaps there was one thing…

He watched the brunette uncurl and stretch lazily and began to walk back to the bed.

Exactly fifty-one minutes later he strode into Sforza headquarters in Rome, wearing an immaculate navy suit and a deep blue shirt, his five o'clock shadow neatly trimmed.

'Mr Sforza!' Carmelina, the junior receptionist, gave a squeak of surprise.

'Carmelina!' he replied, smiling calmly.

'I—I wasn't expecting you in today, sir—' she stammered. 'I must have made a mistake. I thought it was—'

'My birthday?' Massimo laughed. 'It is. You didn't make a mistake, and I'm not planning on hanging around. I just thought I'd pop into the boardroom on my way to lunch at La Pergola. Don't worry! I'm a big boy now. I can wait until tomorrow for my present from the staff.'

He watched Carmelina blush. She was sweet, and clearly had the mother of all crushes on him, but he never mixed business with pleasure. Nor would he—unless there was a sudden global shortage in the number of beautiful, sexually imaginative women eager to share his bed.

He paused briefly in front of the door to the boardroom and then pushed it open. There was a sudden flurry of people pushing back chairs and standing up as he walked purposefully into the room.

'Mr Sforza!' Salvatore Abruzzi, the company's chief accountant, stepped forward, a nervous smile upon his face. 'We weren't—'

'I know.' Massimo waved him away with an impatient hand. 'You weren't expecting me.'

Abruzzi smiled weakly. 'We thought you might be otherwise engaged. But please join us—and happy birthday, Mr Sforza.'

Around the table, his colleagues murmured their congratulations too.

Massimo slid into his seat and gazed calmly around the boardroom. 'Thank you, but if you really want to give me something to celebrate then tell me when we're going to start work in Sardinia.'

There was a strained, simmering silence.

It was Giorgio Caselli, his head of legal affairs, and the closest thing Massimo had to a friend, who cleared his throat and met his boss's gaze. 'I'm sorry, Mr Sforza, but I'm afraid we can't give you that information at the moment.'

For a moment, the room seemed to shrink as though the air had been sucked out of it and then Massimo turned and stared unwaveringly at the lawyer. 'I see.' He paused. 'Or rather, I don't.' He gazed slowly around the room, his blue gaze colder than an Arctic ice floe. 'Perhaps somebody would care to explain?' Frowning, he leaned back in his seat and stretched out his long legs. 'You see, I was led to believe that all objecting parties had been—' His eyes narrowed. 'Removed.'

There was another strained silence and then Caselli raised his hand. 'That's what we believed too, Mr Sforza. Unfortunately the tenant of the Palazzo della Fazia is still refusing to accept all reasonable offers. And as you are well aware, she is legally entitled to stay on at the property under the terms of Bassani's will.'

Pausing, Caselli tapped loudly on the top of a document box on the table in front of him; several of the junior board members jumped.

'Miss Golding has made her feelings completely clear. She's refused to leave the *palazzo*—and, to be perfectly honest, sir, I can't see her changing her mind any time soon.' He sighed. 'I know you don't want to hear this, but

I think we might have to think about some sort of compromise.'

Seeing his boss's set expression, Caselli sighed again and tipped over the box. There was a muffled gasp from around the table as Massimo stared coldly at the sprawling pile of identical white envelopes. Each one was franked with the Sforza logo. All of them were unopened.

He lifted his head, his expression suddenly fierce, his eyes the darkest ink-blue. 'That's not going to happen.'

Now the accountant cleared his throat. 'I think on this occasion, sir, that Giorgio is right. Perhaps we might consider some form of conciliation—'

Massimo shook his head. 'No!' Leaning forward, he picked up one of the envelopes, his face blanked of emotion, the intensity of the gaze belying the quiet reasonableness of his tone. 'I don't compromise or conciliate. *Ever.*'

The eyes around the table stared at him with an unblinking mixture of fear and awe.

'But we've tried every option, Mr Sforza.' It was Silvana Lisi, his head of land acquisitions. 'She simply won't acknowledge our communications. Not even in person.' She exchanged a helpless glance with her colleagues. 'She's completely uncooperative and volatile too, apparently. I believe she threatened to *shoot* Vittorio the last time he visited the *palazzo*.'

Massimo surveyed her steadily. 'How volatile can some little old lady be?' He shook his head dismissively. 'Look! I don't care how old she is, or whether she looks like his *nonna*, Vittorio is paid to acquire land and properties. If he wants to care for the elderly, I suggest he looks for another job.'

His face pale with nerves, Abruzzi shook his head. 'I'm sorry, Mr Sforza. I think you must have been misinformed. Miss Golding isn't a little old lady.'

Lounging back in his chair, Massimo frowned. 'I thought she was some elderly Englishwoman?'

An awkward silence spread across the room and then Caselli said carefully, 'There *was* someone living at the *palazzo* when we first bought the estate—but she was a friend of Bassani, not a tenant, and she left the property over a year ago.'

'So she's irrelevant.' His boss's face darkened. 'Unlike the *volatile* Miss Golding, who appears to have single-handedly thwarted this project and run rings around my entire staff. Perhaps she should be working for me.'

Caselli gave a strained smile. 'I can only offer my apologies…' His voice trailed off as he saw the look of impatience on his boss's face. Sweeping the envelopes off the table, Massimo leaned forward.

'I own that *palazzo*, Giorgio. I own the estate and the land surrounding it. And we've had approval for the first stage of the project for nearly six months and yet nothing is happening. I expect more than an apology, Giorgio—I want an explanation.'

Hastily, the lawyer shuffled through the papers in front of him. 'Aside from Miss Golding, everything is on schedule. We have one or two more meetings with the environmental agencies. Just formalities, really. Then the regional council in two months. And then we're done.' He cleared his throat. 'I know we have permission to convert and extend, but we could just modify the plans and build a brand-new *palazzo* on some other part of the site. We'll have no problem getting it passed, and it would mean we can bypass Miss Golding entirely—'

Massimo stared at him, the cold blue of his eyes making the temperature in the boardroom plummet abruptly. 'You want me to change my plans now? To modify a project we've worked on for over two years because of one tricky tenant? No. I think not.' Shaking his head, he glanced angrily around the room. 'So who exactly *is* this mysterious Miss Golding? Can someone at least tell me that?'

Sighing, Caselli reached into a pile of folders on the table in front of him and pulled out a slim file. 'Her name is Flora Golding. She's English. Twenty-seven years old. She's moved around a lot, so there's not much detail, but she was living with Bassani until his death. Apparently she was his "muse".' The lawyer stared at his boss and smiled tightly. 'One of them, anyway. It's all there in the file.' Caselli licked his lips 'Oh, and there's photographs. These were taken at the opening of the Bassani Wing at the Galleria Doria Pamphili. It was his last public appearance.'

Massimo gave no indication that he had heard a word of this explanation. His eyes were fixed on the photographs in his hand. More particularly they were fixed on Flora Golding. She was clinging to the arm of a man he recognised as the artist Umberto Bassani, and looked far younger than twenty-seven.

She also appeared to be naked.

He felt suddenly dizzy. Wrenching his gaze away, he took a shallow breath and then felt his cheeks grow warm as he saw that she was wearing a dress of some sort of unbleached silk, perhaps a shade lighter than her skin. Noting the soft curves of her breasts and buttocks beneath the clinging dress and the triangle of pale gold skin at her throat, he drew a breath, feeling lust uncurling in the pit of his stomach.

She most definitely was *not* a little old lady!

He studied her face in silence. With that disdainful tortoiseshell cat's gaze and crooked crop of fine brown hair, she was an arresting, unorthodox beauty. But she *was* beautiful—there was no denying that.

A muscle flickered in his jaw as he studied the photo-

graph intently. Beautiful and greedy. Why else would a
woman like that surrender her body to a man more than
twice her age? Suddenly he tasted bitterness in his mouth.
She might look the part, clinging on to her lover's arm, her
eyes lit with an oh-so-convincing adoration, but he knew
from personal experience that appearances could be deceptive. More than deceptive! They could be damaging
and destructive.

Staring down into those incredible tawny brown eyes,
he felt a spark of anger. No doubt a steely will lay beneath
the misty softness of their expression. That and a gaping
hole where her heart should be. His anger shifted into
pity. But what man was truly going to care what lay beneath that satiny skin and curving flesh? And, although he
might have been one of the greatest artists of his genera-
tion, Umberto Bassani had still been just a man. A sick,
elderly, lovestruck fool.

His face hardened. This girl must be quite something if
she'd been willing to hook up with a dying man. A lot more
than something if she'd lured him into letting her stay on
in his home. He felt suddenly sick to his stomach. But was
her behaviour so surprising, really? After all, who knew
better than he how low a woman like that was prepared to
sink in exchange for a share of the spoils?

Or a footnote in a will.

He snapped the folder shut. At least Bassani had had no
children. Whatever Miss Golding's malign influence had
been over the old man, it had now run its course. Slowly,
he ran a finger over the clean lines of his neatly trimmed
stubble. Soon her little protest at the *palazzo* would be over
too, and then denuded of her former powers, she would be
homeless and destitute.

Looking up, he studied the faces of the men and women
seated around the table. Finally he said, almost mildly,

'Perhaps you're right. Maybe we do need a new approach with Miss Golding.'

Clearly surprised by this volte face, Lisi nodded nervously. 'We could use an intermediary.' She glanced at her colleagues for support. The lawyer nodded. 'I think distancing ourselves might be the solution. There are several companies here in Rome that specialise in these sort of negotiations. Or we can go farther afield—London, maybe—'

'That won't be necessary,' Massimo said softly. 'We already have someone working for the company who's more than capable of convincing Miss Golding that our way is the only way.'

Giorgio frowned. 'We do? Who?'

Massimo stared at him calmly. 'Me!'

There was a shocked silence and then Giorgio leaned forward, his forehead corrugated with confusion. 'As your lawyer, I would have to advise you against such a course of action. Let's do what Silvana suggested and find an intermediary. It won't take long but it would be better to wait...' His voice faded as his boss shook his head slowly.

'I've waited long enough. And you know how I hate waiting.'

'But, sir.' Giorgio's face was taut with shock. 'You really shouldn't get personally involved. This is business—'

'Yes. *My* business. And it involves me personally.'

'I understand what you're saying, sir, but I really don't think it's wise for you to meet Miss Golding—' The lawyer stopped, clearly horrified by the prospect of his uncompromising boss actually coming face to face with the shotgun-carrying, volatile Miss Golding. 'Anything could happen!'

Massimo felt his body stir. *Yes. It could!* His eyes flickered over the photographs of Flora, inexorably drawn to the beauty of her body and the challenge of her gaze. His chest tightened. She would be passionate at first, and then tender, those honeycomb-coloured eyes melting as she pulled him fiercely against her...

Closing his mind to the tantalizing image of a naked, feverish Flora, he smiled and the tension around the table evaporated like early morning mist.

'Don't worry, Giorgio. I'll be sure to wear my bullet-proof vest,' he said.

His lawyer grimaced and slumped back in chair. 'Fine. You can meet her. But only if I'm there to make sure you don't say or do anything you or more importantly *I* will regret!' He shook his head in frustration. 'I would have thought that you would have had something better to do, today of all days.'

Massimo pushed back his chair and stood up smoothly. 'I do indeed. I have a surprise birthday luncheon waiting for me at La Pergola.' His eyes gleamed beneath their dark brows. 'Reschedule it for this evening! That should give Miss Golding more than enough time to sign on the dotted line. And now you and I have a helicopter to catch.'

Two hours later, Massimo closed his laptop with a decisive click. The file on Flora Golding had made an entertaining read, but she hardly offered anything in the way of a challenge. In his experience pretty, greedy young women simply needed the correct handling to help them towards the sticky end they so richly deserved.

Leaning back against the plush upholstery, he stared at the Tyrrhenian Sea through the window of his private helicopter. Away from the coastline the water gleamed flat and bluer than a gemstone, while in the distance he could just make out where the waves lapped against the island's famous ragged granite outcrops.

He turned as the pilot leaned forward. 'Beautiful scenery isn't it, sir?' he shouted over the whirring buzz of the helicopter's rotors.

Massimo shrugged. 'I suppose so.' He glanced down at his watch and then shifted round to face the lawyer who sat, eyes squeezed tightly shut, his face damp with sweat.

'Open your eyes, Giorgio. You're missing the scenery,' he said mockingly. Frowning, he shook his head. 'I don't know why you insisted on coming. You know you hate flying. Just take deep breaths and we'll be back on terra firma before you know it.' He turned back to address the pilot. 'How long before we land?'

'Ten minutes, sir.'

Massimo frowned. 'That was quick!'

The pilot grinned. 'We made good time—but then this chopper's the best on the market.'

Massimo nodded. To him, the helicopter was simply a means of transport. He had no interest in the make or model. Nor did its stupidly high price tag excite him. In truth, all of his 'toys'—the cars, jets and luxury yachts— left him cold. What truly excited him was the pursuit of some unattainable deal. He loved going head to head with an opponent. And the more he—*or she*—tried to outmanoeuvre him, the more single-minded and ruthless was his desire to bring them down.

As Miss Flora Golding was about to find out.

The pilot pointed out of the window. 'That's the Palazzo della Fazia, sir. If you don't mind, I'll probably bring her down over there.' He gestured towards a large, flat patch of land at the end of the drive.

Massimo nodded, but his eyes were fixed on the honey-coloured building in front of him. The helicopter touched down lightly and as the rotors slowed, he stepped onto the parched grass, his gaze continuing to rest on the *palazzo*. He owned many large and impressive properties, but he found himself holding his breath as he stared at the golden stucco shimmering beneath the Majorelle blue sky. He was transfixed not by its grandeur but by its serenity and its sense of reassuring immutability—as though the building had grown up out of the land itself.

'Thank goodness that's over!'

Massimo turned sharply as Giorgio came and stood beside him, patting his pallid, sweating face with a handkerchief.

'How are you feeling?' he asked drily.

The lawyer smiled weakly. 'I feel okay.'

Massimo frowned. 'Really? You look terrible. Look... Why don't you wait here? I don't think you being sick in the flowerbeds is going to help close this deal, do you?'

Giorgio opened his mouth to object. Then took one look at his boss's face and closed it again.

Massimo smiled. 'Don't look so worried. This won't take long.'

The driveway definitely needed some attention, he thought critically, as he sidestepped a crater-like pothole. Up close, the *palazzo* too had clearly seen better days. Parts of the stucco were crumbling, and there were small plants poking through the plaster like loose threads on a jumper. And yet still there was something magical about its faded glamour.

He scowled, irritated by this sudden and wholly uncharacteristic descent into sentimentality. There was nothing magical about bricks and plaster. Especially when they were reduced to rubble. And as soon as Miss Flora Golding signed over her tenancy rights that was exactly what was going to happen.

Eyes narrowing, he climbed up the steps to the large front door and pulled purposefully on the bell rope. Tapping his fingers impatiently against the brickwork, he frowned and then pulled on the rope again. There was no answering jangle from inside and stifling a stab of irritation, he hammered hard against the peeling paint, resting his hand on the wood, the heat of it somehow feeding his anger.

Damn her! How dare she keep him waiting like this? Craning his neck, he looked up at the first-storey windows, half expecting to see a face, the eyes dancing with malice. But there was no face, and for the first time he realised that the windows—*all* the windows—were shuttered. Gritting his teeth, he straightened up. The message could hardly be clearer: Miss Golding was not at home to visitors. *Ever.*

His head felt full to spilling with rage. Turning on his heel, he walked down the steps and strode along an untidy path beside the *palazzo*, his shoes crunching explosively on the gravel. Each shuttered window seemed to jeer at him as he passed, and his anger swelled with every step. Reaching the end of the path, he found a gate, the latch broken and with what looked suspiciously like a woman's stocking tied around it to keep it shut. Irritably, he tore at it with his fingers.

Stalking past a pile of discarded masonry and rusting iron railings, he felt a quiver of excitement as he stepped through a crumbling stone archway into a walled garden. In contrast to the front of the building, all the shutters and the windows at the back of the building were open, and then, turning towards the *palazzo*, he noticed a half-empty glass of water and the remains of an apple on a marble-topped table. So she *was* here! But where, exactly?

Blinking in the sunlight, his spine stiffened as he got his answer. Somewhere in the gardens, a woman was singing.

He stared fiercely around the *terrazza*, but it was empty except for a handful of sunbathing salamanders. For a moment he was rooted to the spot, the pounding of his heart drowning out the song, and then, forcing himself to breathe more slowly, he lifted his head. But it was too late. She'd stopped singing.

Damn it! He turned slowly on the spot, his eyes narrow slits of frustration. Where the hell *was* she? And then he heard it—the same husky voice—and he felt another flicker of excitement. With light, determined steps, he ducked under an archway festooned with roses—and then stopped almost immediately. It was just another empty terrace. His disappointment aching like a blow to the stomach, he glanced through a fringing of leaves at a large sunken ornamental pond and a collection of marble nymphs.

What the hell was wrong with him? Chasing after a singing girl like some foolhardy sailor bewitched by a siren…

And then his breath stopped his throat and his heart seemed to miss a beat as across the garden he saw one of the nymphs reach out to touch a cluster of pale pink oleanders.

Dry-mouthed, he watched her bend and twist in silence, his breath still trapped somewhere between his throat and his stomach. With the sunlight gleaming on her wet body she looked like a goddess fresh from her morning bath. Her beauty was luminous, dazzling. Beside her the exquisite marble nymphs looked dull and blandly pretty.

Staring hungrily at the slender curl of her waist, the small upturned breasts, he felt the blood start to pulse in his neck. His eyes followed the soft curve of her backbone down to the firm, rounded bottom. The vertebrae looked both defenceless and dangerous and he watched, silently mesmerized as she lifted her arms, and stretching languidly, began to hum. And then his breath almost choked him as he saw that she wasn't completely naked but was wearing a tiny flesh-coloured thong.

The scrap of damp fabric tugged at his gaze.

His chest tightening, he stared at her hungrily, his blood pulsing thickly as she dipped her feet into the pond and then began to sing again in the same sweet, light voice.

Massimo smiled. He recognised the song, and with the breath spinning out of him like sugar turning to candy-floss he started to whistle the tune.

The girl froze, her head jerking upwards. Taking a step forwards, she frowned. 'Who's there?'

Moving out from under the archway, Massimo held his hands out in front of him. 'Sorry. I couldn't resist. I hope I didn't scare you.'

She stared at him fiercely, and he realised with surprise that she didn't seem scared. Nor had she made any attempt to cover her nakedness. But then given the beauty of that body, why should she? His own body hardened painfully as she looked up at him defiantly.

'Then perhaps you shouldn't creep about in the bushes. This is private property and you're trespassing. I suggest you leave now before I call the police.'

Her Italian was fluent, and bore no trace of an English accent, and he felt another stab of surprise and admiration too. But neither showed on his face as he smiled at her coolly.

'The police! That might be a little premature.' His English was perfect and, watching her eyes widen with surprise, he smiled grimly, gratified to see that he had got under that delectable skin. 'Don't you want to know who I am first?'

'I know who you are, Mr Sforza.' Her voice was clear and calm. She lifted her chin. 'And I know what you want. But you're not going to get it. This is *my* home, and I'm not about to let you turn it into some ghastly boutique hotel for loud, sweaty tourists, so you might as well leave.'

'Or what?' His eyes drifted casually over her naked breasts. 'If you're concealing a weapon, I'd really like to know where.' He stared at her mockingly. 'This is *my* property and *my* land and you are *my* tenant. As your landlord, I'm entitled to inspect what's mine. Although, to be fair, I think you've pretty much shown me everything there is to see.'

Flora glared at him, her eyes flashing with anger. So this was the famous Massimo Sforza—or was that infamous? The man whose arrogant swirling signature had dominated her days and dreams for so many weeks. He was everything she had imagined him to be: slickly clever, charming yet ruthless. But now, with that glittering blue gaze locked onto hers, it was clear she had underestimated the ratio of charm to ruthlessness. Meeting his eyes, she felt a shiver of fury run through her body. He clearly believed that his presence was dazzling enough to overpower her objections to his stupid hotel. If so, he was sadly mistaken. She'd had her fill of men simply assuming that she would fit in with their plans. Particularly one as smug as Massimo Sforza.

Her heartbeat began to quicken. He *was* completely, irredeemably loathsome. So why then was her pulse fluttering like a moth near a candle? Heat burned her cheeks and she shook her head in denial—but there could be no denying her body's treacherous, quivering response to his. Nor the fact that he was the most wickedly attractive man she'd ever met.

And the most dangerous.

She gritted her teeth, confused and angered by her body's response. It was so inappropriate and shallow and given who she knew him to be, frankly *wrong*. So what if he was handsome? Hadn't she seen his photo in enough newspapers and magazines to have grown sick of that sculpted head? Her body felt hot and taut beneath the intensely blue focus of his gaze, but she shivered. It was crazy: he hadn't even touched her. But nothing could truly have prepared her for the reality of his beauty or that air of power and self-assurance. With that sleek black hair, the flawless bone structure just visible beneath the stubble and that imperious gaze he might easily have been one of the bandits that used to roam the island's hills.

She scowled. Only now, instead of robbing rich travellers of their money and jewellery, he robbed ordinary people of their homes and livelihoods. He might be wearing the trappings of respectability and wealth—his suit and shoes were clearly handmade and expensive—but he had the morals of a common thief.

Her gaze skipped swiftly over the breadth of his chest. It might be broad—but not because he was big-hearted. This man didn't have a heart, and she would do well to remember that the next time she got dewy-eyed about his blatant masculine perfection.

'I didn't have you down as a prude, Mr Sforza,' she snapped back. 'Not given your well-documented fondness for scantily clad women. But then it doesn't surprise me in the least that you're a hypocrite. After all, you are the head of a multinational corporation—so it's sort of a prerequisite, isn't it?'

Massimo shrugged casually, but the intensity of his gaze made her breathing jerk. 'I'm not a prude. You caught me off guard. You see I don't generally discuss business with naked women. But then I don't tend to frequent strip joints.'

Her eyes glittered brighter than the Sardinian sun. 'I'm *not* a stripper,' she said frostily. 'And we are *not* doing business. This is my home and I can walk around in it any damn way I want.' She paused, her face twisting with scorn. 'Besides, unlike *some* people, I don't have anything to hide.'

Her pulse leaped as his face darkened with anger.

'Oh, you think nudity equates to honesty, do you? Interesting. In that case, I've got nothing to hide either.' Eyes glittering, he slid off his jacket and tossed it disdainfully onto a nearby rose bush, showering petals in every direction.

'Hey!' Flora took an angry step towards him. 'What the hell do you think you're doing?'

He glanced at her and instinctively she tensed as she saw the hostility in their cobalt depths. 'Me? I'm showing you the purity of my soul.' Holding her gaze, he slowly began undoing the buttons on his shirt.

She gritted her teeth. 'Really? You're *really* going to do this?'

Flora stared at him helplessly. This couldn't be happening. Surely he wasn't going to take all his clothes off in front of her just to prove a point? She watched in silence, a knot forming in her stomach, her heart beating frantically as he tugged his shirt off and threw it on top of his jacket. Meeting her gaze, he pushed his belt through the buckle and undid the top button of his trousers.

'No!' Turning round, she grabbed a faded sundress from the stone slabs and pulled it over her head in one swift moment.

'And I thought *I* was the prude!'

She heard the note of triumph in his voice and turned to face him with wide, scornful eyes. 'Not wanting to see you naked doesn't make me a prude. It's just a matter of taste. I know you must find it hard to believe, but I don't actually find you attractive enough to want to see you naked.'

'Oh, I can believe that. I'm clearly a little young for your taste. Perhaps I should come back in thirty years.'

Flora frowned. 'Thirty years?' she repeated stupidly. 'Why would that make any difference?'

Massimo shook his head. 'Don't play the innocent with me, *cara*. We both know I'm rich enough for you. But you like your men *old* and rich, don't you, Miss Golding? Or should that be Miss Gold-Digger?

Her eyes blazed with fury. 'How *dare* you?' She stepped towards him, her hands bunching at her sides. 'You know nothing about my relationship with Umberto.'

Her stomach muscles clenched, the knots inside pulling tighter. He was disgusting! A monster. Coarse, cold-blooded and corrupted. How could she have thought he was attractive? And he was such a hypocrite! Barging into her life and her home and judging her like that. Her breath felt sharp in her throat. Not just judging, but destroying something good and pure—sullying the memory of what had been innocent with his vile insinuations.

Scowling, she lifted her chin. Let him think what he wanted. She knew the truth. That she and Umberto had shared not passion but friendship, and a mutual desire to hide: she from her family's claustrophobic love and he from the knowledge that his artistic powers were fading.

'Just for the record, I don't have a problem with your age. Just your character! Umberto was twice the man you could ever hope to be, and you will never be capable of understanding what we shared. But it certainly wasn't his bank account.'

He smiled coldly. It was the smile of someone to whom such an outburst was a sign of weakness and imminent surrender. 'The lady doth protest too much. Although in your case...' he raised his eyebrow mockingly '... I think "lady" might be pushing it somewhat, don't you?'

Leaning over, he picked up his jacket and reached into the inside pocket. He pulled out an envelope and held it out to Flora.

'Save your self-justification for someone who cares.' His face hardened. '"Just for the record", I don't care who you sleep with or why. I just want you out of here— and, despite your damning little speech about my character, I think if you look inside that envelope you'll find that I understand pretty much everything about you, Miss Golding.'

His icy, knowing smile made her stomach flip over. She glared at him but he held her gaze.

'I like playing games as much as the next man, *cara*, but you don't have to play games with me anymore. And this *is* a game, isn't it? You holding out for more and me giving you what you really want?'

She stared at him in silence. His blue eyes were as deep and tempting as the Tyrrhenian Sea.

'Come on, *cara*,' he said softly. 'Umberto was a rich man, but accept my offer and you'll be a far richer woman.'

Flora stared at the envelope in silence. A rich woman! She could almost picture the cheque: could see that authoritative swirling signature.

He watched with grim satisfaction as she hesitated momentarily and then took it from him. 'Aren't you going to open it?'

She looked up at him, hating the note of triumph in his voice. 'No,' she said quietly, her eyes fixed on his face. And then with slow deliberation she tore the envelope in two and threw it at him. 'I don't need to. You see, there's nothing you can offer me that I will ever want. Except never to see your vile, arrogant face again!'

And before he even had a chance to reply she turned and darted through an archway and vanished as a light breeze blew the pieces of envelope and cheque across the flagstones.

CHAPTER TWO

MASSIMO STARED AFTER her in confusion. What the hell had just happened? Had she really just taken his cheque and ripped it up? Without even looking at it?

His stomach contracted. Everything he'd wanted had been almost in his grasp and now he felt stupid and out of place—almost as though she'd left him standing at the altar, with the pieces of envelope fluttering around his feet like discarded confetti. His breathing quickened. *Damn her!*

'Mr Sforza?' At the sound of Giorgio's voice he turned sharply. Looking pale and flustered, his lawyer hurried across the flagstones. 'I'm sorry I took so long. This place is like a maze. But I heard voices.' His eyes popped slightly as finally he seemed to register his shirtless boss, and then he looked quickly away. 'Er…is everything okay? I mean—'

Massimo's face darkened. He was well aware of how he must look, standing there half-naked and alone like some spurned suitor. His confusion was gone, replaced by a rage so pure, so absolute, that it seemed to fill his entire body.

'Everything is fine,' he snapped. 'I just thought I'd have a quick sunbathe.'

The lawyer gazed at him uncertainly. 'Really…?'

Massimo shook his head in exasperation, his body seething with a frustration that took him straight back to his childhood. 'No, Giorgio. Of course not. I was—' Grimacing, he shook his head again. 'It doesn't matter.' Breathing out slowly, he picked up his shirt and slid his arms into it. 'You can tell Lisi she was right, though. She *is* volatile.'

'That's the impression I was given, sir.' Giorgio nodded, a look of relief sliding over his face. 'That's why I think we should cut our losses and walk away before...' He glanced furtively across at his boss, who was buttoning up his shirt with swift precision. 'Before this gets any more out of hand.'

Massimo whirled towards him. 'Walk away?' Snatching up his jacket, he shrugged it on carelessly, his voice colder than marble. 'Oh, I've got no intention of walking away, Giorgio. Not before I've taught Miss Golding a long and clearly overdue lesson in manners. Come with me.'

He turned and began to walk swiftly in the direction that Flora had just taken. Ducking under the archway, both men came to an abrupt stop as they emerged onto a neatly trimmed grass lawn. Across the lawn a high yew hedge rose out of the ground, in the centre of which was another archway. There was no sign of Flora—

'This is getting ridiculous,' Massimo muttered. 'How many gardens does one *palazzo* need?'

They crossed the lawn and stopped in front of the archway. It wasn't a garden.

'It's a maze!' Giorgio gazed uncertainly at a small rusting sign. He looked up at his boss, his expression a mixture of astonishment and dismay. 'Do you think she's in there?'

Massimo scowled. Of course she was in there. No doubt laughing her pretty little head off at their expense.

He sighed. 'I should have ripped the damned house down with her in it. I know I said this before, but I'm going to sort this out once and for all and then I'll be back. And this time I really won't be long. After all, how difficult can it be to find her?'

The answer to that question was *really* difficult, he decided some twenty minutes later, after he'd turned yet another corner to find yet another dead end. With a groan of frustration, he ran his hands through his hair and cursed Flora loudly.

'I may not be a lady, but even *I* wouldn't use words like that!'

His body froze as her voice, fizzing with malice, cut sharply through his tirade.

'What's the matter, Mr Sforza? Don't you like hide and seek? I thought you liked playing games "as much as the next man".'

He spun round, his gaze boring into the thick, dark leaves. 'Oh, very funny. This is very amusing, I'm sure. But you can't hide from me for ever!'

'Probably not! But I've got a funny feeling that after an hour...' she paused, and sighed elaborately '...or *four* spent wandering around in here, you might just want to go home. If a bullying, greedy monster like you actually *has* a home.'

He gritted his teeth and then his pupils flared as from somewhere behind the high green hedge, he heard a twig snap. *Gotcha!* Slowly, with delicate steps, his heart hammering with excitement, he crept towards the end of the path and stepped swiftly around the corner. But there was no one there.

'You might as well give up and go home.'

Her voice floated through the foliage, the crisp, cool words acting like salt on his wounded pride. And yet despite his irritation part of him was enjoying this game they were playing.

His mouth curved into an almost-smile. 'If you knew me better, *cara*, you'd know that I never give up or give in.'

'Thankfully I will never know you at all. Anyway, carry on looking if you want, but I should warn you there's over a thousand metres of paths and only one of them will take you to the centre. Still…happy hunting!'

Massimo glanced up at the sky, and his breathing slowed. She was going to pay for this. And a lot sooner than she thought. Reaching into his trouser pocket, he pulled out his mobile phone and punched in a number.

Flora stared up at the thick, yew bushes and felt a surge of satisfaction. The maze had been designed by Umberto and had a particularly fiendish layout. Massimo Sforza would be stuck wandering around between its high, impenetrable hedges hopefully until the sun set. She smiled happily. Which should give him ample time to ponder the ethics of harassment and bribery.

Her smile faded. His casual, unfounded assumption that her reason for staying at the *palazzo* was to squeeze more money out of him and his stupid company made her skin tighten with anger.

If only there was some way to get rid of him for good. But like most rich, powerful men, he was used to getting his own way.

She felt suddenly tired. Was it so much to ask to keep her home? But it was always the same. Even reasonable, well-adjusted men seemed to assume that a woman could and should change her life to fit in with their plans.

Remembering James's angry disbelief when she'd refused to upend her life for his, she felt an ache spread inside of her. And it had been the same with Thomas too. He'd been bewildered and then furious with her for pursuing her own goals instead of supporting him.

Her lip trembled. Then of course there was her dad and

her brother, Freddie. They'd always been *protective* but since her mother's death, they'd treated her like she was a child; an adorable but foolish child who needed protecting from herself.

Still, at least they loved her and cared about her. Massimo Sforza, on the other hand, only cared about himself. But just because he was rich and used to getting his own way didn't mean she should give up her home so he could turn it into a stupid hotel.

She shivered. The stone bench on which she'd taken refuge was cold, and even though the sun was gleaming like a huge pearl in the flawless blue sky the seven-foot hedges meant that little of its heat was reaching her.

Damn Gianni! It was all his fault. If only Umberto hadn't left him the estate. And if only his feckless, greedy brother hadn't sold it on as soon as the deeds were in his hands, she wouldn't be here, hiding like a criminal on the run.

A twig cracked nearby, and she froze momentarily—then relaxed. It was probably just a lizard or a bird. Massimo Sforza might be rich and powerful but he'd need x-ray vision or wings to find her in here.

Her head jerked up abruptly. Above her, a Marsh harrier gave a shrill screech and, frowning, she slid off the bench, a shiver of apprehension scuttling down her spine. It might have been muted by the hedges, but it had definitely been a warning call. But before she could even ponder as to what might have caused the bird's alarm she heard a faint droning noise, and then a shadow fell across her upturned face and the droning become a loud rhythmic 'whumping'.

Open-mouthed, Flora stared up in astonishment at a large, sleek white helicopter. Where had it come from? And then she gave a sudden cry of rage. *Sforza!* It had to be. She'd assumed he'd driven to the *palazzo*, but who else would have such a showy boy's toy? She must have been swimming under the water in the pond when he'd flown over—

There was a crunch of footsteps on gravel behind her, and her heart leaping in her chest, she turned, knowing before she did so that it would be him.

'Thanks, Paolo. Yeah, I think I can find my way out. But I'll call you if I need your help.' Massimo clicked off his phone and examined her face, his eyes glittering with malice. 'So. We meet again.' He glanced at his watch and frowned. 'Not quite fifteen minutes!'

'Only because you cheated!' Hands curling into fists, Flora stepped backwards. Her calves collided painfully with the stone bench, but it was nothing compared to the injuries she would inflict on Massimo if she stood too close to him.

He shook his head. 'You're not going to have a tantrum about losing, are you, *cara*? I told you—I don't give up and I don't give in. And, besides, I hate waiting.'

She shivered as his face shifted, grew harder and colder than the marble bench pressing against her legs.

'And I never, *ever* lose.'

Flora stared at him stonily. 'What a wonderful mantra for life. Your parents must be so proud of you.'

His eyes flared, and nervously she realised that his broad body was blocking her only way of escape.

There was a short, tense silence and then he shrugged. 'And what about *your* parents, *cara*? Were they proud that their daughter was shacked up with a man old enough to be her grandfather?' He paused, his lip curling, his teeth bared so that for a moment he seemed to resemble a large, dangerous animal more than a man.

She lifted her chin and met his gaze. 'We can stand here all day and trade insults, if you want,' she said stiffly. 'But it won't alter the fact that I have a legal right to stay here as a tenant for as long as I wish. Nothing you can do or say will change that fact.'

For a long moment he stared at her steadily and then, to her astonishment, he smiled without rancour. 'That's true.'

She waited tensely as he continued to study her, his abrupt change of mood almost as unsettling as the growing realisation that they were only inches apart, alone, separated from the rest of the world by seven-foot hedges. Goosebumps tiptoed over her skin, and she swallowed uneasily. Why was he looking at her like that? It reminded her of the way buyers used to look at Umberto's paintings: cool, assessing, critical.

She shivered again, and he frowned slightly. 'You're cold! Of course, you must be.'

Before she could reply, he had pulled off his jacket and draped it over her shoulders. His hand grazed her skin, and she shivered once more, this time from the heat of his touch.

Feeling somehow disloyal—although to what or to whom, she wasn't sure—she tried to shrug it off, but he shook his head.

'It's just a jacket, *cara*. Not a white flag.'

Blushing, wondering how or when her thoughts became so transparent, she nodded mutely. She felt hot. Impatient. Restless. But where had all her anger and outrage gone? Wrapping her arms tightly across her chest, she stared mutinously past his head. *He* was making her feel like this. His tantalising nearness seemed to have driven all rational thought from her mind. And now, wearing his jacket, with the warmth of his body still clinging to the fabric, she felt even more confused.

Still staring straight ahead and desperate to at least appear cool and calm, she cleared her throat. 'I'll walk you out.' His gaze was burning her skin and, turning, her heart shivered as her eyes collided with his.

He nodded slowly. 'Then I won't charge you for the loan of my jacket.' Her eyes widened and he grinned. 'I'm kidding. Look. I can find my own way out—'

She rolled her eyes. 'No you can't. Come on. It'll only take a few minutes.'

It took seven. Giorgio was waiting at the entrance. He glanced anxiously at their faces. 'Ah, there you are. There you *both* are—'

Massimo interrupted him smoothly. 'Giorgio. I don't believe you've met Miss Golding. Miss Golding, this is my chief legal advisor, Giorgio Caselli. Our business is done here, Giorgio. I'll see you back at the helicopter.'

Looking both astonished and respectful, the lawyer nodded. 'It is? Excellent. Wonderful. It was a pleasure to meet you, Miss Golding.'

Flora stared after him, a sense of foreboding creeping over her skin. Was that it, then? After all these months of harassment, was he just going to give up and walk away?

She turned to face him. 'I don't understand. Are you saying I can stay? Or is this some game? Because I don't know how to play.'

His mouth curved at the edges. 'This isn't a game.'

'But it doesn't make any sense,' she replied fiercely. 'One minute you're jack-booting around like some crazed dictator on a rampage, and now you're being—' She stopped.

'What? What am I being?'

His blue eyes were fixed on her animated features and she frowned. 'I don't know—reasonable, nice!'

He winced. 'Reasonable! *Nice?* I don't think anyone has ever accused me of being that before!' His tone was teasing.

'I don't suppose they have,' she said cautiously.

He grinned, his handsome face softening. 'It's a low blow! *Arrogant, ruthless, crazed*...I can handle. Niceness, though... That's dangerous! Whoever heard of a *nice* CEO?'

She bit her lip.

He frowned. 'I'm serious. You have to promise me: what happens in the maze, stays in the maze. I can't have my reputation as a "bullying, greedy monster" ruined.'

Recognising her words, Flora blushed. 'You were a bit bullying,' she said carefully. 'But I suppose that doesn't matter now.'

He was watching her thoughtfully. 'I'd like to think it doesn't.' Pausing, he glanced across the lawn. 'Are there more gardens over there?'

Surprised by the change of subject, she nodded.

'I'd like to see them. Will you show me?' he asked simply.

Breathing in the drifting scents of blossom and warm earth, Massimo was surprised—impressed, even—by the scale and diversity of the gardens. He was no horticulturist, but even he could see that in stark contrast to the *palazzo* it looked as though someone was taking care of them.

Between narrow gravel-filled paths edged with meticulously trimmed bay hedges, the neat, square beds were filled with lavender, thyme, rosemary and sage, while espaliered fruit trees mingled with climbing roses, jasmine, honeysuckle and wisteria on the walls and arches.

Massimo ran his hand lightly over a topiary spiral. No doubt Bassani had taken up gardening when his career as an artist had begun to fade. Squinting into the sunlight, his face tightened. It was pretty, but gardening—like all hobbies—seemed a complete waste of time to him. He worked out with a personal trainer five mornings a week, but work fulfilled all his needs except rest and relaxation, which was why, in his leisure time, he liked to sleep and have sex.

His lip curled—although not necessarily in that order.

'It's beautiful,' he said finally. 'I didn't know Bassani was such a keen horticulturist.'

Flora looked up at him, her mouth curving into a pout, and he felt his groin tighten almost imperceptibly. How to describe those lips? Not red, not pink— He smiled grimly as the words came to him from school art lessons: *rose madder*. He stared at her critically. A tiny scar just above her eyebrow and a sprinkling of freckles over her nose and cheeks contrasted with the classical symmetry of her face and saved her from being just another pretty girl. But that mouth was a work of art: a mixture of challenge and seduction, determination and—surrender.

An image of Flora, soft-eyed, her body melting against his, those lips parting, exploded inside his head.

Struggling to keep himself from touching the plump cushion of her lower lip, he gestured offhandedly towards a cluster of dark red peonies. 'Did he choose everything?'

Flora shook her head slowly. 'Umberto didn't have anything to do with the gardens—' She checked herself. 'He liked sitting in them, of course, but he knew absolutely nothing about plants.' She wrinkled her nose. 'He couldn't tell a weed from a wallflower!'

Watching her eyes mist over as she talked about her lover, Massimo felt something twist inside him. The thought of Flora and Umberto together, her bewitching young body pressed against the older man's, made him want to snap the heads off the flowers—

Her voice broke into his thoughts. 'He sometimes helped me with the planting, though. Not the actual digging, but he always knew what plant should go where. I think that's

because he was an artist; he had a wonderful eye for colour and composition.'

Massimo nodded. 'I know even less about colour and
composition than I do plants. But I have a couple of properties on the mainland,' he said idly. 'I could do with a capable gardener.' His blue eyes gleamed. 'Maybe I could
poach yours.'

She burst out laughing. He was impossible. Incorrigible. Infuriating. And for one bizarre moment, it actually
felt like they liked each other. Biting her lip, she met his
gaze. 'So now that you can't have my home, you want my
gardener?'

Amusement lit up his eyes. 'I hadn't thought of it like
that but—yes. It seems only fair.'

The gentle, mocking tone of his voice made her heart
beat faster. He was still her enemy, she told herself frantically. He was a devil in disguise and she shouldn't let
her guard down just because his eyes were like woodland
pools and his voice was as sweet and silken as wild honey.

'That's not going to happen,' she said carefully, hoping
that her face revealed nothing of her thoughts. 'Looking
after these gardens—' she frowned 'Well, it's not just a
job. It's more complicated than that.'

His eyes were dark and teasing. 'Compared to that maze
nothing is complicated! Don't look so worried, *cara*, I'm
not going to kidnap your gardener. I can see you don't want
to lose his services.'

Their eyes met, and she felt her skin grow warm and
tingling beneath his lingering gaze. His eyes were a beautiful, deep, dark blue of a forget-me-not, and she felt a sudden sharp heat inside as she stared at his lean jawline and
the full, passionate mouth. He would be impossible to forget even if his eyes *didn't* demand that he be remembered:
his lean, muscular body, the compelling purposefulness of

his gaze and the intensity of his masculinity set him apart from every other man she'd ever met. And his smile— She felt a rush of longing. What woman *wouldn't* want to be the cause of that smile?

And then, as though the sun had gone behind a cloud, his smile faded. 'I'm sorry,' he said slowly. 'It must be the heat or something. I'm usually a little quicker on the uptake.' He frowned. 'You don't have to explain. I get it.'

'Get what?' The hair on the nape of her neck rose at the sudden tension between them.

'Obviously, he's a "friend" of yours.'

She stared at him, confused. 'Who?'

'Your gardener.'

The expression on his face was hard to define, but she could almost see him retreating, and she felt a rush of panic. 'He's not a friend of mine. I mean, he can't be. He doesn't exist,' she said breathlessly. '*I* do the gardening. *Me*. On my own.'

There was a moment's silence as he studied her face and then he smiled slowly, and once again she felt her nerves flutter into life and her skin grow warm. 'Is that so? You really are full of surprises, Miss Golding. No wonder Bassani was so smitten with you!'

There was nothing new in his words. She had heard them said in so many ways, so many times before. Normally she let them wash over her, but for some reason she didn't want this man to think that they were true.

'No—it wasn't like—' she began but her words stopped in her throat as he reached out and gently took her hand in his. Turning it over, he ran his fingers lightly over the hard calluses on her palm, and she felt her breath snag in her throat; felt heat flare low in her pelvis. Her heart was racing. She knew she should tell him to stop, should pull her hand away, but she couldn't speak or move.

Finally, he let go of her hand and said softly, 'So. This is why you want to stay.'

It wasn't a question, but she nodded anyway. 'Yes. Partly.'

She looked up at him hesitantly. She never talked to anyone about her real work. Most people on the island simply assumed that she was Umberto's muse, and it was true—she *had* often posed for Umberto. But she'd only modelled for him as a favour. Her real passion, ever since she was a little girl, was flowers, although not many people took her seriously when she told them—probably because they were too busy pointing out the fact that her name was Flora and she liked flowers: a joke which had stopped being funny years ago.

She took a deep breath. 'I'm actually writing a thesis on orchids. The island's home to some very rare species. That's why I came here in the first place.' Feeling suddenly a little shy, she gave him a small tight smile. 'I didn't even know about the *palazzo* or Umberto before I arrived. I just bumped into him in a café in Cagliari.'

Massimo studied her assessingly. She made it sound so innocent, so unplanned. As though her relationship with Bassani had been a matter of chance. His face hardened. Yet here she was with her name on the tenancy agreement. He gritted his teeth. However she spun the story, he knew she had been looking for some sort of sugar daddy, and in Sardinia there was only one man who fitted the bill.

A muscle flickered in his jaw. Women like Flora Golding did their homework. Nothing was left to chance. Because if their efforts succeeded then, like his stepmother Alida, they need never work again—although spending his father's money had pretty much been a full-time job for *her*. His body stilled as he allowed himself a brief memory of his stepmother's icy disdain, and then he gazed coolly at Flora.

No doubt she'd found out where Bassani had liked to drink and set the whole thing up. He could well imagine the older man's greedy excitement on discovering this beautiful young girl sipping cappuccino in some shabby little bar. And then all she'd had to do was pose for him. Naked. At the thought of Flora slipping out of her faded sundress, her eyes dark and shiny with triumph, he felt almost giddy with envy and lust.

For a moment he lost all sense of time and place, and then he breathed out slowly. 'How fortuitous,' he said smoothly. 'To find your own blank canvas here at this *palazzo*—the very place you have chosen to make your home.'

He stared broodingly across the garden, blind to its beauty. He should have been satisfied by this final proof that she was as disingenuous and manipulative as he'd suspected, but beneath the satisfaction was an odd sense of disappointment, of betrayal. And of anger with himself for responding to her obvious physical charms.

His jaw tightened. But wasn't it always so with women? Especially women like Flora Golding, who had duplicitous charms ingrained in them from an early age. *Flora.* It was a name that seemed to suggest a honeyed sweetness and an unsullied purity. And yet it tasted bitter on his tongue.

His gaze sharpened as she looked up at him, her light brown eyebrows arching in puzzlement at the shift in his voice. 'I do love the gardens, but it's more of a hobby than anything else. My real work is my dissertation and if I'm going to finish my thesis I need peace and quiet. And that's what I get living here.'

Massimo smiled. Her tone was conversational, her words unremarkable, but she had unwittingly given him the means to her end.

They had reached the front of the *palazzo*. Abruptly he

turned to face her. 'It's been an enlightening visit, Miss Golding. Don't worry—we won't be contacting you anymore. And there certainly won't be any more financial incentives. You've made it perfectly clear that you're not motivated by money, and I respect that.'

Flora blinked in the sunlight. Even though the day was now suffocatingly hot, she felt a chill run down her spine. His voice sounded different again—almost like a sneer or a taunt. But nothing had changed. Maybe it was just the heat playing with her senses…

'Good,' she said quickly, trying to ignore the uneasiness in her stomach. 'I'm just sorry you had to make a personal trip to understand how I feel.'

He stepped forward, and she felt a spurt of shock and fear for this time there could be no confusion. His face was cold and set.

'Don't be. I always like to meet my enemies face to face. It makes closing a deal on my terms so much easier.'

It took a moment for the implication of his words to sink in. 'Wh-what deal?' she stammered. The word echoed ominously inside her head. 'There *is* no deal,' she said hoarsely. 'You said so. You said you wouldn't be contacting me or offering me money again.'

He smiled coolly, a contemplative gleam in his blue eyes. 'I won't. You won't be getting a penny of my money. Not now. Not ever.'

She stared at him, chilled by the undisguised hostility of his gaze. 'I don't understand…' she began, but her words died in her throat as he shook his head.

'No. I don't suppose you do. So let me make it clear for you. Like I said earlier, *cara*, I *always* get what I want.' His face seemed to be no longer made of flesh and blood, but cold stone. 'And I want you out of here. Normally I'd pay, but as money's not an option I'm going to have to use some other method to get what I want. But believe me I will get it. And by the time I've finished with you, you'll be begging to sign any contract I put in front of you for free.'

She stared at him, her heart pounding against her ribs. 'What do you mean?' But already he had begun walking down the drive. 'Y-you're wrong! Y-you can't do anything!' she called after him. 'This is my home!'

She was panting, stuttering, her anger vying with her fear. He was bluffing. He had to be. There was nothing he could do.

But as she watched the helicopter rise up into the sky and slowly disappear from view she knew that it was she who was mistaken. She had thought he had come to the *palazzo* simply to broker a deal. And maybe it had started out that way. But that had been before she threw his deal back in his face. She felt a rush of nausea. Now there would be no more deals, for his parting words had been a declaration of war. And she knew with absolute certainty that when Massimo Sforza came back next time he would be bringing an army.

CHAPTER THREE

ROLLING OVER IN her large wrought-iron bed, Flora stared miserably out of the window at the cloudless sky. She'd slept badly again. Her night had been filled by images of Massimo Sforza, his eyes darker than his bespoke navy blue suit, beckoning her towards him only for the floor to open up beneath her feet.

Her cheeks grew warm, and she shifted uncomfortably beneath the bedclothes. The nightmares had been horrible, but the dreams were far more unsettling. Dreams of a naked Massimo, his lean, muscular body pressed against hers, those long, supple fingers drifting lazily over her skin and—

And what? Irritably, she sat up. He'd probably take the bed, with her still in it, and push it out to sea—and frankly she'd deserve it.

Gritting her teeth, she pulled on a faded black T-shirt and a pair of sawn-off jeans and stomped downstairs. Holding her breath, she forced herself to look at the letter cage hanging on the back of the door, but there was no heart-stopping white envelope to greet her, and she breathed out slowly.

It had been three weeks since Massimo had turned up at the *palazzo*, but still she sensed his presence everywhere. The thought that someday she would turn round to find him standing there, watching her, his face rapt and triumphant, made her feel dizzy.

But only until the anger kicked in.

In the kitchen, she took out a plate and a cup and glanced up at the deadbolts she'd fitted to the French windows. As a tenant, she was forbidden from changing the main locks, but there was nothing in her contract about adding additional security so she had bought new solid steel padlocks for all the gates too. Glancing up at the old iron range, she felt the tension inside her ease a little. There was only one key to the huge, solid oak front door and it was hanging there, between the skillet and the espresso coffee pot. Whatever happened, Massimo Sforza was not going to be able to barge his way unannounced into her home again.

She woke the next morning to the insistent ringing of her mobile phone. 'Okay, okay,' she mumbled, fumbling on the bedside table, her eyes still screwed shut. 'Hello? Hello!'

Opening one eye, she squinted into the sunlight filtering through the gap in the curtains. Who the hell was ringing at this time? And, more importantly, why weren't they saying anything? She gazed irritably at her phone and then her breath seemed to freeze in her lungs as the ringing began again—from somewhere downstairs.

For a moment she lay gripped with confusion, panic swelling inside her, cold and slippery as a toad. Wishing her heart would stop making so much noise, she strained her ears. Surely she'd imagined it—but there it was again. And then from nowhere came a high-pitched screeching that made her press her hands over her ears.

Still wincing, she rolled out of bed. She wasn't scared now. Burglars didn't use drills. She sniffed suspiciously. Or make coffee!

The noise downstairs was even louder than in her bedroom. Edging into the kitchen, she took a deep breath as her mouth fell open in horror. Everywhere she looked, there were people in overalls and boxes piled on top of one another.

Her lips tightening, she tapped the nearest man on the shoulder. 'Excuse me! What are you doing in my kitchen?'

But before he could answer a woman with a sleek shoulder-length blond bob, wearing a clinging grey jacket and skirt, slid past her, miming apologetically.

Gritting her teeth, Flora gazed furiously in front of her. She might not go shopping much anymore, but she knew a designer suit when she saw one and that little outfit probably cost more than her food bill for a year.

It also answered her question more eloquently than any workman could have done.

Her face twisting with anger, she stormed out onto the *terrazza*. 'I *knew* it,' she spat. 'I knew you'd be behind this! You are such a—' She swore furiously in English at the man lounging at the table, drinking coffee.

He frowned, his handsome face creasing with mock horror. 'Somebody got out of bed the wrong side.' His eyes gleamed maliciously. 'Good morning, Miss Golding! I hardly recognise you with your clothes on!'

'Ha-ha! Very amusing. Now, will you please tell me what the hell you're playing at?'

'I'm not *playing* at anything, *cara*. This is work.' His eyes pinned her to the spot. 'I'm sorry we got you up so early, but not all of us have the luxury of a lie-in.'

He was speaking in English too, and she stared at him mutely, trying to work out why. And then abruptly he stood up and languidly stretched his shoulders and all rational thought went out of her head as her body went on high alert.

'Don't mind us,' he said, stifling a yawn. 'We can just carry on down here and you can go back up to bed.'

Flora gaped at him. Why was he acting like this? He

was being friendly, pleasant. He was making it seem as though this was something she'd agreed to. Glancing round, she felt her skin grow warm as she saw two of the men on his team share a conspiratorial glance.

Did they think she and Massimo were—? She opened her mouth to protest—and then stopped as Massimo smiled malevolently at her outraged expression.

Their eyes met and his smile widened. 'Actually, I had a very early start. Perhaps I'll just come up with you—'

She glowered at him. 'No. You will not—' And then she jumped violently as a loud thumping started from somewhere further inside the house. 'What the *hell* is that noise?' Turning, she stalked back into the kitchen like an angry cat.

Following her, Massimo shrugged, his face bland and unreadable. 'I'm not exactly sure.' He gestured vaguely towards a box of cables. 'Something to do with improving the internet.'

His eyes picked over the two spots of colour on her cheeks and the pulse throbbing in her neck and something in their considering gleam made her want to take some of the cable and strangle him with it. But instead she gritted her teeth. Knowing him, he was probably hoping she'd do just that so he could exercise some medieval right to remove unstable female tenants.

She took a deep breath. 'You can't do this, Mr Sforza—'

'Call me Massimo,' he said smoothly. 'I know I'm your landlord, but there's really no need to stand on ceremony.'

She bit her lip—he was baiting her. Worse, he was enjoying watching her struggle with her temper. 'Yes. You are my landlord. Which means that you can't just walk in here whenever you feel like it.'

'You know, I thought you'd say that,' he murmured, reaching into his jacket pocket. 'So I had one of my staff print off a copy of your tenancy agreement. Here. You can keep it.' He glanced at the slanting pile of letters stacked against the wall. 'File it with all your other important documents.'

Staring at him mutinously, she snatched it from him. 'I don't need a copy. I know what it says, and it says that you can't just turn up without warning. You have to give me notice.'

He frowned. 'Did I not do that? How remiss of me. I can't imagine how that happened. And there was me, trying to be a good landlord—'

'You were not,' she retorted, her resolve to keep her temper hanging by a fibre optic thread. 'If you were, your men wouldn't be bashing holes in my walls—they'd be fixing the roof and the plumbing. You're just doing this to try and make my life difficult. So why don't you just take your stupid internet cable and all this other rubbish and leave before I call the police?'

He held her angry gaze, and she saw that flecks of silver were dappling his eyes like sea foam. Her heart began to thump painfully.

'Why bother?' he said easily, glancing at his watch. 'I'm meeting the Chief of Police in an hour for lunch. We're old friends. I can mention your concerns to him, if you like.'

The expression on his face was hard to define, but whatever it was it didn't improve her temper. 'Which presumably he'll then ignore?' she snapped. *Damn him!* Pretending he was concerned about her when they both knew the exact opposite was true.

'There's no need to get hysterical, *cara.*' There was a glint of satisfaction in his eyes. 'I'm only trying to help you.'

It was the last straw. Her voice rose shrilly. 'You're not trying to help anyone but yourself.'

He took a step towards her and held out his hands apologetically, placatingly. 'I am. Truly. And I'm sorry about all this noise and mess.' Turning, he barked out a few words in rapid Italian, and as if a switch had been flicked the hammering and drilling stopped and within seconds the kitchen was empty and silent.

She stared at him, confused.

'Here. Drink this.' He held out a glass of water and then as she took it, he shook his head and said softly, 'You see. You're already starting to wish you'd taken the money, aren't you?'

For a moment she floundered, shocked by his malice and sheer bloody-mindedness, and then anger, hot and damp like wet earth, rose in her throat. Breathing out slowly, she put the glass on the table. She wanted to kill him.

'Is that why you're doing all of this?'

He shook his head. 'No. I'm doing all this for my new tenant. Your new neighbour.'

She gaped at him. '*What* new neighbour?'

'The new tenant who's moving in today. It was in the email.' He paused. 'The one that wasn't sent.' He smiled blandly. 'Don't look so worried. I hand-picked him myself.'

It took all her will-power not to throw the glass of water at his head. Finally, she said flatly, 'Let me guess. He's a drummer in a band. Or maybe he breeds huskies or budgerigars.'

He laughed. 'Are you saying I'd *deliberately* pick an antisocial tenant to make your life hard?' He shook his head. 'Sorry to disappoint you but there's no dogs or birds. Just a nice, quiet businessman.'

Something wasn't right.

His words nudged each other inside her head and then she knew what it was. She went hot, then cold, and then hot again with horror.

'No!' She shook her head, her pupils flaring. 'No! You are *not* moving in here. You can't—'

'But I can.'

He paused, and her pulse soared as he smiled at her slowly—a dark, taunting smile that sent a shiver through her body.

'You're not scared, are you, *cara*? After all, it's a big house.'

She felt a jolt, low down, felt suddenly horribly out of her depth. It was a big house but she knew that he would dominate every inch of it. A lump rose in her throat. It wasn't fair. This house was her home—her refuge from the world. But how was she supposed to feel safe living with a man who looked at her with such absolute focus? Such predatory purpose?

Fear mingling with desire, she stared at him in silence, terrified that he might somehow be able to read her mind as the blue gaze lingered on her hot, flushed face.

Finally, he shrugged. 'I've taken the bedroom next to yours—the blue room.' Pausing, he smiled coldly. 'Of course if you don't like it you can always move rooms. Or move out.'

Her stomach clenched, and she could barely swallow her anger. 'Over my dead body.'

Massimo smiled coldly. Normally his business decisions were based on logic and reason. But his decision to move into the *palazzo* had been driven by pure, elemental rage. Flora had defied him and he'd wanted to punish her defiance—to rub his power in her face.

Giorgio had been appalled. His team astonished. It had been reckless and completely out of character. And yet he'd still gone ahead and done it.

His body twitched and he stared at her greedily, a memory of her near naked body stealing into his mind like a cat burglar. For weeks it had been the same story. He'd found it impossible to concentrate, his mind drifting off, distracted by images of a fierce-eyed Flora melting into his arms—

His breathing slowed. And why not, he thought idly. He'd tried money and threats and reasoning with her and none of those had worked. So why not seduction?

He smiled at her, feeling the tug of sexual tension between them. 'I'd rather be on top of your living one.'

Flora swallowed the lump in her throat. Fear spiked inside her. Until that moment it hadn't been real—this feeling, this longing. It had just been inside her head: private, shameful. Now it was out in plain sight. His gaze rested intently on her face, and she felt something hot and dry eddy over her skin like the air pushed out of a tunnel by an approaching train.

'You're disgusting,' she whispered.

He studied her face fully, his eyes narrowed, knowing, cruel. 'Just honest,' he murmured. His lip curled. 'You should try it some time.'

Her pulse beat loudly in her head; her mouth was dry. What was the matter with her? Was she really so shallow that her body could simply override what her brain knew to be true? Massimo Sforza might be heart-stoppingly handsome, but he was also a despicable human being.

She walked slowly across the kitchen and stopped in front of him. They were so close that she was dizzily aware of the warmth of his body and the scent of lavender and bergamot that clung to his skin. Her heart was hammering in her chest, her eyes huge as she looked up at him.

'You forcing your way into my home is a pretty scummy thing to do—and I'd honestly thought you couldn't sink any lower. How wrong I was! Sorry to disappoint you, but I don't do housework, listen to opera or sleep with men I hate.'

She felt a sting of satisfaction as his smile vanished. After so many months of feeling harried, it felt good to turn on her hunter.

His fine features twisted mockingly. 'Hate? Oh, you don't hate me, *cara*. You're afraid of me. Afraid of how I make you feel.'

They were inches apart, and she found herself staring helplessly at his full and sensuously curved lips. How could a man with so little integrity have such a beautiful mouth? It was cruel and unfair.

'You're right,' she said hoarsely. 'I *am* afraid. Afraid I might get sent to prison for beating you to death. As if I'd sleep with you after how you've treated me! You are literally the most arrogant, insensitive person I've ever met.'

His eyes were cold. He let the silence grow and swell between them until it felt as if it was bruising her.

Finally, he shrugged. 'I don't know why you're making such a big deal of it. I'm not asking you to do anything you haven't done before.'

Her whole body was trembling, as though the fury and outrage inside was trying to burst through her skin. 'Which is *what*, exactly?' she snapped.

He gave her a speculative look. 'Sleep with a rich man to make your life easier.'

With satisfaction he watched something flutter across her eyes even as her hands curled into fists. How far could he push her? And how hard would it be to make her forget her anger and give in to the tension that had been building between them ever since that first day in the garden?

He gritted his teeth. For his sake, he hoped it wouldn't be too long. His self-control was already being severely tested.

Flora felt fury sweep over her skin. 'You're not only

rude, you're wrong. *Your* girlfriends might act like that, but I'm not that kind of woman.'

'Oh, I think you're *exactly* that kind of a woman,' he said softly. 'But don't get me wrong. I'm just making sure we understand one another. It doesn't actually matter to me what kind of woman you are. After all, men and women don't need to like or respect one another to have sex. You of all people must know that.'

She felt her breathing change, anger layering on top of the pain. 'No. They don't. But they have to like and re-spect themselves—and I wouldn't be able to do either if I slept with *you*.'

There was a glint in his eye but his voice was surpris-ingly calm when he spoke. 'As you wish. And now I really *do* have work to do, so enjoy your breakfast.'

He turned and walked out of the kitchen before she had a chance even to register that he was leaving. For a mo-ment, still seething with resentment, she stared after him in stunned silence. And then she shivered. Maybe she should have just taken the money and gone...

Her mouth tightened. But why should she have to give up her home? Whatever he might like to imply, he couldn't force her to her leave. She had the law on her side. And she had the measure of him now.

Stepping out into the garden, she blinked. Only that was proving less of a help than a hindrance—now she knew just what she was up against. Knew that he would use every weapon at his disposal to get his way. Unfortunately what she hadn't realised until now was that his most effective weapon was himself.

Hunched over a tray of seedlings in the greenhouse, Flora blew a strand of hair out of her eyes and, looking up, stared resentfully at the beautiful honey-coloured *pala-*

zzo. It had only been five days since Massimo Sforza had moved into the building but already she knew that he had changed her life. And she was not sure it would ever be the same again.

Her once peaceful home was now filled with a succession of painters and plumbers—and, of course, his glossy-haired, expensively clad entourage. And that was just the men, she thought sourly.

Standing up, she arched her back and let out a long, slow, calming breath. Why did all the women employed by Sforza have to look like extras from a Victoria's Secret show? Surely it couldn't be a prerequisite of working there: that would be vile, not to say illegal. She pursed her lips. Although what would a bit of male chauvinism really matter to a man like Massimo?

Wiping her hands on her shorts, she picked up the tray and slid it into the rack, her face darkening. She'd been determined to ignore his existence, or at the very least treat it with the indifference it deserved. But it was proving hard when everywhere she looked there was some reminder of his presence: a pair of carelessly discarded cufflinks on the kitchen table, a sleek black sports car parked in the drive…

Flora sighed softly. Her life and her home were no longer her own. And there wasn't anything she could do about it.

At least not if her brother was to be believed.

Freddie ran his own law firm in London and, having sat and stewed in a mixture of misery and frustration, she'd finally rung him and given him an edited version of what was happening.

Thankfully, he had a big case on and was more distracted than usual. Unfortunately he'd simply confirmed her suspicions that she had two choices: stay or leave.

But somehow hearing it from him had seemed to snap it into focus.

'The law's on his side,' Freddie had said, the grim note in his voice underlining her plight. 'Technically, he should have notified you...'

He'd paused, and she'd gripped the phone tightly, willing him to present her with some watertight legal argument that would wipe that smug smile off Massimo's handsome face.

'And...?' she prompted, and heard him sigh.

'Not and—but! But it just won't be worth pursuing it. For a start it'll take so long to come to court, and secondly—on paper, at least—he's a good landlord. I mean, you said he's doing all the repairs you wanted.'

Flora stared tiredly down at her bare feet. He was. And some she hadn't even asked him for—like installing a gleaming stainless steel cooker with a baffling array of dials and programmes.

'I'm sorry, Flossie!'

Her brother's use of her childhood nickname made a lump form in her throat.

'It's okay,' she said quietly, kicking a pebble into the sunken pond. 'It was just a thought. And thanks for looking into it. I know it's not your thing.'

She could almost picture the amused expression on his face. 'It's a little domestic for my tastes. But then again, Sforza's a big name. He's high-profile. I could easily stir the pot up a little.'

She sighed. 'No, thank you. I can handle him. It's just nice to know I can run things past you.'

Freddie cleared his throat. 'You know you can always ring me. It makes a nice change from all the usual horror.'

Freddie specialised in 'causes', not cases, but she knew he loved his work.

'Look…'

She heard the shift in his voice.

'I know you don't want to hear it, but you're wasting your time out there. There's plenty of flowers in England too, you know. Why don't you come home? Dad would love to see you. We both would. You can have your own room—'

Gritting her teeth, Flora interrupted her brother quickly. 'Thanks, Freddie. But I'm not leaving the *palazzo*. It's my home—'

But he'd already moved on. 'Okay. But just promise me you're not going to go looking for a fight. Just keep your head down and stay out of his way—'

Glancing at the seedlings in front of her, Flora sighed. Of course she had promised, and she had meant what she said.

She had no intention of giving Massimo Sforza the satisfaction of getting what he wanted, and launching an all-out battle against him would have done just that. He was clever and cool-headed enough to keep on goading her until she snapped—thus giving him the perfect justification to end her tenancy. So, much as she would have liked to take him on at every opportunity, she'd kept her promise and kept out of his way.

She bit her lip. And it was fine. Except that Massimo's arrival in her life had been so sudden, so traumatic, that living with him felt as if she was dealing with the aftermath of some natural disaster. Everything familiar and safe had gone. Now even something simple, like eating breakfast, was so highly charged with possible outcomes that just thinking about it left her exhausted.

At some point she would be happy to resume open warfare, but in the meantime she was like a shipwreck survivor alone on a raft at sea. Picking up another tray of seedlings, she sighed. What she really needed was time to come to terms with her new circumstances. Time to get her bearings. And time to plan her next step...

Thankfully, the following two weeks went by without incident. The house was finally free of dust sheets and ladders, and the smell of wet paint was starting to fade. Much as she had done before Massimo's arrival, Flora spent most of her days in the greenhouses, writing up notes for her thesis. And after a couple of days spent looking warily over her shoulder she'd finally begun to relax, for it was clear that whatever occupied her landlord's days it didn't involve venturing into what she thought of as *her* space.

The gardens, though, represented a somewhat trickier prospect. A sort of no man's land. It was galling to admit it, but she skirted round them to reach the greenhouses. However, she couldn't avoid going there for ever unless she was happy to see them all go to seed. Picking up her favourite trowel and a pair of secateurs, she shut the greenhouse door firmly. She would start today with the rose garden. It always needed the most attention.

Her cheeks grew warm. The fact that it was the garden farthest away from the *palazzo* obviously had nothing to do with her decision.

After days stuck in the greenhouses, it felt glorious to feel the sun on her skin and hear the birds chattering excitedly in the hedges. The air was thick and heavy: there would be a storm later, but probably not until the evening. She worked steadily, only stopping to eat a makeshift lunch of a *sebadas* and some grapes.

Finally straightening up, she noticed a beautiful apricot floribunda: Absent Friends. She had planted it after Umberto died. He had loved all roses, but that delicate coral colour had been his favourite.

'You poor old thing,' she said softly. Brushing the petals lightly with her hands, she inhaled the smooth, voluptuous scent with pleasure. 'I'm sorry I've haven't been looking after you.' Gently, she trimmed back a couple of straggling stems. 'There. That's better!'

Smiling, she turned to throw the discarded blooms into her bucket—and it was then that she saw Massimo's tall figure, leaning casually against the stone sun dial that formed a centrepiece to the rose garden.

'I've heard of people talking to their pets. Or even to trees. But I've never heard anyone talk to a flower before.'

Slowly, he began to walk towards her, his eyes fixed on her face. Hypnotised, she watched him come closer, her body stilled by the sudden tension in the air. Even the birds had fallen quiet, their sharp cries replace by a taut, expectant silence.

He stopped in front of her, and she felt suddenly almost giddy. After so many days of harbouring a grudge against him it was a shock to see him again. And a greater shock to be reminded of how beautiful he was. Her eyes skipped nervously over the curved, hard muscles of his arms and chest. Dressed casually in blue jeans and a faded grey T-shirt, he looked more indie rock star than autocratic billionaire businessman.

His gaze travelled lazily over her and despite the warmth of the day she felt a shiver trickle over her skin.

'So. Do they talk back?'

He spoke gently, without any hint of mockery, but she still felt her cheeks grow warm.

She gripped the roses tightly. 'Sometimes.'

The sun seemed to light up the bones beneath his skin, emphasising the finely etched features, the firm jaw and smooth, slightly angular cheeks. There was strength there, and a compelling authority, but also restraint—as though he were holding something back...some dark energy. Quickly, she looked away.

'What are they saying now?'

His voice was so cool and clear that it made her feel thirsty. Somewhere inside her head a warning bell was ringing faintly in time to the beating of her heart. He was too close, and suddenly her breath caught in her throat, hot and panicky, as around her the birds broke into sweet, high song and a trembling breeze shook the leaves on the bushes.

He alone was silent, watching her with eyes so deep and blue she thought she might drown in them.

Trying to ignore her heart thumping against her ribs, she cleared her throat. 'They're saying, *Why is this really annoying man trampling all over us?*'

Their eyes met, and her skin twitched, and heat flared in her stomach as his lips curved into an irresistible smile.

'Really? I thought they were saying, *Why did this really annoying woman cut off our heads?*'

'So you think it's *my* fault you trod on them? That somehow *I'm* responsible for your actions?'

He laughed softly. 'Definitely. That's what nymphs do, isn't it?'

She felt her cheeks flood with colour. 'I am not a nymph. And no, it is not what they do. They simply personify nature.'

'That's what all nymphs say. Right before they bewitch some helpless man with their beauty.'

He was teasing her, and those ridiculous eyelashes were flickering like sea anemones in a rock pool. Breathing in slowly, she tried to frown; tried her hardest not to respond to the dizzying pull of his smile but she couldn't resist.

'And that's you, is it? You're the helpless man?' She lifted her chin. 'Why didn't you say that in the first place?'

Massimo felt lust gnawing at his body. He thought himself a man of the world—if not debauched then occasionally decadent—but he didn't think he'd ever seen anything as erotic as Flora, wearing a loose T-shirt cinched at the waist with an old brown leather hunting belt, her bare feet pressing into the earth.

Her cheeks were flushed, and he studied her face, watching her dimples deepen. She was teasing him, testing him. And for a moment he forgot all about punishing her. He even forgot that he wanted her to move out. In fact, her leaving was the last thing on his mind. Like a child running to reach the sea, every inch of him was focused on one goal: getting her to surrender that delectable body to him.

Her eyes were exactly the colour of cinnamon, hinting at warmth and sweetness. And a whisper of fire. He felt his groin tighten. She would be like that in bed. Sweet and warm...that incredible lush pink mouth melting beneath his...those even white teeth nipping and biting in ecstasy—

'I didn't want you to take advantage of me.'

Flora swallowed. The garden was warm; the droning sound of insects soporific. But even though his eyes seemed drowsy, she knew he was watching her intently, and the heat on her back felt suddenly like a warning. A reminder that Massimo was not and never would be helpless and that it was he who was distracting and bewitching *her*.

Slowly, she turned to drop the dead roses in the bucket and then, trying to keep her voice steady, she said, 'I'm pretty much finished here. I should probably go and clean up...'

Her heart gave a lurch, her words petering out as slowly he stepped towards her. 'Wait!'

It was a command, not a request, and she wondered if

he ever relinquished his power to anyone. His eyes were the same blue-black as the storm clouds gathering on the horizon and she stared at them as though mesmerised, a pulse fluttering in her throat. Being near him was so confusing. She felt surrounded—overwhelmed, almost and yet she wasn't scared or suffocated by his power.

Like a bee seeking pollen, his gaze settled on her lips and suddenly the humming of her blood threatened to blot out the warning voices in her head.

'We should go inside. It's going to rain,' she said hoarsely. 'Can't you feel it?'

He smiled—a dazzling smile that made her heart split— and she felt a quiver of panic. How could something be so irresistible and yet so dangerous?

'Are you sure that's what it is?' he said softly.

Mutely, she stared at him, and then she felt heat flare up inside her as gently he reached out and stroked her hair. 'Wh-what are you doing?' she stammered.

'I'm checking to see if you're real.'

'Why wouldn't I be real?'

She felt his fingers move. 'Because you've got petals in your hair,' he murmured, holding out his hand to show her. 'And you're dressed like some woodland nymph.'

His gaze on her face was blunt and she felt her cheeks grow warm.

'I'm just a gardener.' Her voice was husky, her eyes both fierce and afraid. 'You, on the other hand, have been out in the sun too long if you think I'm some nature goddess. You should get inside.'

Shaking his head, he stepped closer—so close she could see the flecks of brilliant cobalt in his eyes.

'You'll have to do better than that. If you want me to leave then tell me and I'll go.'

She swallowed. 'I want you to leave,' she lied.

There was a moment of silence and then he nodded. 'There. That wasn't too hard, was it?'

The air seemed to tremble between them, and relief and regret and merged inside her.

'You see. We're both liars.'

And slowly he lowered his head and tilted her face up towards his. Her heart seemed to drop inside her and she felt suddenly glutted with longing, and the rightness of that longing, and the heat of that longing. The breeze and the birds fell silent and still and her breath stopped. And then like a diver on a springboard she curled her toes into the grass and, standing on tiptoe, kissed him gently.

Fire flooded her skin and the tension inside her that had been growing and growing burst as his mouth moved softly over hers. She felt his tongue drift teasingly over the curving flesh of her lips and, moaning softly, maddened by its firm, probing tip, she kissed him more fiercely, nipping his mouth with her teeth.

His fingers slid slowly over the nape of her neck and then her lips parted in surprise as he jerked her against him, his arms tightening around her slender body as he deepened the kiss. Helplessly, she arched herself against him, the heat of his body drawing out the heat inside her—a relentless, tugging, pulsating thread of longing and need.

She was losing herself; she felt breathless, euphoric. Her hands slid over the broad muscles of his back, caressing the hard body beneath his shirt. Her blood was singing, her nerves dancing in time to the frenzied beating of her heart. And then she heard him groan, and her stomach clenched in a sharp, almost painful spasm.

Hazily, she became aware that her skin, her dress, his hair was wet. Abruptly, she pulled away. Eyes wide, she stared at him dazedly, and then tugged her dress back onto her shoulder.

Massimo's expression was a mixture of frustration and amusement as raindrops splashed lightly onto his face and shoulders. 'It's only rain, *cara*!'

She smiled weakly. 'This is a bad idea. We should go inside.'

Her voice was breathy and uneven. For a moment he said nothing, just watched her in silence, making no attempt to hide either his desire or his triumph.

Finally, he nodded. 'I agree. Your bedroom or mine?'

CHAPTER FOUR

THERE WAS A SHORT, strained pause. For one brief, dizzying moment, Flora imagined his fingers curled round hers, imagined them running through a merry-go-round blur of hedges and walls, their feet moving up the stairs…

And then her skin grew cool. A shiver rose up her spine and her eyes widened in angry disbelief. 'What are you talking about?' she said slowly.

Your bedroom or mine? Had he really just asked her that question? His arrogant assumption that, having kissed, she would simply go to bed with him jarred inside her like an out-of-tune piano.

'Do you actually think we would—?' She stared at him incredulously. 'You are *unbelievable*.'

Like war paint, the leaves of the rose bush cast stripes of shadow across his face. His eyes were narrow, angry and thwarted.

'For wanting to have sex with you? I'm a man and you're a woman and we just kissed like the world was about to end. Of *course* I'm going to think about sex.' His eyes glittered. 'And you kissed me first, so I don't really know what you were expecting—'

'I didn't expect anything! Why should I? Nothing happened!'

'Nothing happened?' he ground out, his voice cold with fury. 'You call that *nothing*?'

She glanced up at the sky. Above them, a rainbow was shimmering, its gentle pastel arcs somehow at odds with the sharpness of his anger.

'No. I call it a mistake. One I don't intend to repeat.'

A faint blush suffused her cheeks and throat. She couldn't deny the heat humming in her veins. Or the fact that she had responded to him with a force and intensity that had never happened with any other man. But he wasn't just 'any other man'. He was the cold-hearted, manipulative man who wanted to make her homeless and she would have to be a certifiable lunatic to forget that for the sake of one kiss.

She glared at him. 'I don't have to explain myself to you. And as I only sleep with men I like and respect, I'm not going to have sex with you either. But I guess that's where you and I differ. Your standards are probably a little lower than mine.'

His face felt taut; the blood was pounding in his ears like a battle drum. He couldn't believe she'd turned him down. Had she any idea how many women would jump at the chance to sleep with him? His anger was slick and hotter than blood.

'A lot lower. They pretty much hit rock bottom a moment ago.'

Flora's heart thumped dully in her chest. The contempt of his tone as much as his actual words left her breathless, chilled. 'You're a pig,' she said shakily.

He studied her face, his mouth forming something between a smile and a sneer. 'I prefer pragmatist. As far as I'm concerned I don't need to like or respect a woman to want to have sex with her. And I want to have sex with you. Just as much as you want to have sex with me. Except you're too much of a hypocrite to admit it.'

Heat burned her cheeks. 'You're not only disgustingly arrogant, you must be deaf too! I already told you that I don't want to have sex with you.'

Something flickered across his face—subtle but deliberate and designed to goad.

'My hearing's perfect, *cara*. You told me you wouldn't sleep with me because you didn't like or respect me. You never said you didn't *want* to. As for the arrogance—I guess I *was* a little presumptuous. But only because I have cause to be. Women *like* me.'

She shook her head incredulously. 'No. They like your money!'

'Are you speaking from experience?'

His taunting smile made her want to drop the sun dial on his head. 'Fine. Have it your way. Every woman you've ever met wants to have sex with you.' She paused, her eyes flashing with anger. 'Until now! But don't take it personally. It's not as if I have to like or respect a man *not* to want to have sex with him.'

His eyes hardened. 'You're a very good liar, Miss Golding. Plenty of practice, I suppose? But that's the trouble with telling lies. You stop being able to recognise the truth. And the truth is that you want me like I want you. And pretending otherwise isn't going to change anything.'

His words were still ringing in his ears. Was that the truth? With shock, he realised it was. That using sex to gain her trust no longer seemed as important as ridding himself of this debilitating haze of sexual frustration.

She stared at him. His words had blunted her power of speech, their sharp, undeniable truth slicing through her skin down to the bone.

He studied her coolly, long enough for her to know that he knew exactly what she was thinking, and then lifting his gaze, he squinted up at the sky. 'Anyway, I'll leave you to your flowers—' his eyes gleamed '—and your righteous indignation. But let me know *when* you change your mind.'

There was a pulsing silence, and then he turned and walked calmly away without waiting for a reply.

A bubble of hysteria rose up inside her. 'You're wrong, Massimo Sforza!' she shouted. 'I don't want you and I never will.'

As she watched him disappear beneath an archway she shivered, feeling both the chill of his absence and the rapidly sinking sun. Pressing her hands against the cool stone of the sun dial, she breathed out slowly. Those few febrile moments in Massimo's arms had convinced her that having sex with him would not just be a mistake. It would be a disaster. And not because of who he was. But because of how he had made her feel for those few vivid moments.

She bit her lip. It was embarrassing to admit it, even to herself, but she wanted him. With a longing that was as hot and as real as the sun. But it wasn't lust or even shame that was making her feel like a startled deer. Something had happened even before his fingers had slid over her skin. Something new and unsettling and yet also familiar. Something that had made her heart ache and then start to race like a sprinter. That teasing banter, that soft encircling warmth of his smile had been a reminder of what two people could share.

Her face tightened. *And lose.*

Looking up, she stared at the arch of colours shifting and fading into the thunderous sky. Massimo Sforza was more than just a temptation. He was dangerous: a flashing red sign, a shrill, warning cry. And to ignore that fact would be like running towards the edge of a cliff in pursuit of a rainbow. Her independence, the sanctuary of calm isolation that was her life in Sardinia, these were solid and real and reliable. And she needed to remember that next time she felt like getting up close and personal with her landlord.

Massimo strode through the gardens, his gaze fixed on the path ahead of him, currents of confusion and anger tugging him sharply over the stone slabs and the gravel of the drive. Heat was pulsing out a telegraph of dots and dashes over his skin. The same message over and over again.

What the hell had just happened?

Sliding into the driver's seat of the black Lamborghini slung carelessly across the driveway, he forced his breathing to slow and tried to pull his thoughts into focus. And shift the painful throb of his erection.

She'd kissed him. And he'd kissed her back. And a kiss was just a kiss. So why the hell did it feel as though a hole had just opened beneath his feet?

It made no sense. Flora Golding was a nobody. Up until a few days ago she had been nothing more than a name— a glitch in his plans to make Sforza Industries the biggest hotel and resort company in the world. But now—

A memory of Flora, lips parted, eyes drowsy with desire, slid into his head and a teasing twist of lust spiralled lazily inside him. His heart throbbed in his throat. Glancing down at his hands, he saw that they were shaking, and he felt a spasm of fury at this sudden and uncharacteristic loss of control.

What was the matter with him? It was bad enough behaving like some adolescent schoolboy. But he couldn't shake the feeling that something had happened in that garden. Something more than mere sexual attraction. Something too blurred and just out of reach.

Gritting his teeth, he shook his head.

What was it about this skinny English girl with messy

hair and eyes like an angry cat? Even before he'd met her in the flesh she'd been messing with his head. Playing games. Pulling strings.

And he'd let her.

Even though he'd vowed never to let it happen again. Never to let his emotions rise up and drag him under to that place of dark misery that had been his childhood.

His stomach tightened as it always did at the thought of his stepmother and, grimacing, he pressed the ignition, letting the snarl of the engine override the jerky beat of his heart. He'd let that manipulative little witch get under his skin. But it wouldn't happen again. Whatever it was he thought he'd felt when he held her in his arms was just that: a thought. Fleeting, illusory—like a rainbow.

Shifting gear, he imagined the day ahead. He had a meeting with the architect. Then lunch with his land agent. Maybe afterwards he would take the yacht out. Invite a couple of 'guests' to join him. Find a deserted beach and lose some inhibitions.

Feeling calmer, he pressed his foot down lightly on the accelerator pedal. The hard stone of fear and doubt inside him was disintegrating, mingling with the dust whipped up from the road, and as he pushed the car up a gear, his head emptied of everything but the sound of the engine and the intoxicating rush of air.

'And six of the tomatoes, please.'

Flora gazed dully at the colourful fruit and vegetables spilling onto the dusty ground. She wasn't a keen cook, preferring meals of almost rustic simplicity, but this was one of her guilty pleasures: poring over the crates of lemons and artichokes in Cagliari market.

She had woken early and, hounded by the memory of what had happened the day before, had slipped out of the *palazzo* with no plan in mind other than avoiding Massimo. Now, wandering aimlessly around the town, she felt both listless and strangely on edge.

Crossing the road towards the café quarter, she felt a sudden sharp pang of envy as a pair of teenage boys shot by her on a scooter, shouting with laughter. Yesterday she had felt like that too: carefree and unfettered. But now everything had changed.

And it was all because of him: *Massimo.*

She bit her lip. It was so unfair! And irrational!

It wasn't as if she'd never been kissed before. She'd had boyfriends. Actual, real-life boyfriends whom she'd liked and respected. Her cheeks grew warm. Only their kisses had never felt like that.

Even now she could still feel the touch of his lips on hers, vivid and blazing like a brand. And, more worryingly, she couldn't stop thinking about what he'd said to her after she'd kissed him. It had been arrogant and crass and it should have repelled her. But it hadn't. Instead, she had felt something stir inside her—a tingling, flickering tug of desire that had tasted warm and sweet and smooth on her tongue—

She took a hard, fast breath and, stopping abruptly in front of a café, sat down and ordered a coffee. A folded newspaper had been left on the table and she threw it onto the unoccupied chair beside her, dropping her bag on top of it.

Glancing round at the smiling, happy faces, she felt a pinprick of fear. Surely there had to be rules about this sort of thing. It didn't make sense that he, of all people, should have such an intense physical effect on her. She bit her lip, goosebumps tingling over her skin. But was it really that incomprehensible? Massimo Sforza was the most beautiful man she'd ever met. Sexy and smart, and of course arrogant beyond belief. But nothing could detract from his dazzling, wild, mesmerising beauty.

Her phone buzzed inside her bag and, relieved to have an excuse to push away her unsettling thoughts, she pulled it out. Her relief faded and her breath jerked in her throat. It was Freddie.

Typically, he started speaking as soon as she picked up. 'I think you're right. You should stay put.'

Flora frowned. Her mind seemed to have stalled. Had Freddie just told her she was *right*? 'Okay...' she said hesitantly. 'Wow! That's great. It feels like the right thing to do. I mean, I can't just up and leave every time something gets tricky. Sometimes you have to stay and fight—like Spartacus.'

'So you're saying you're like a slave in Ancient Rome?'

Freddie's voice was pleasant enough, but the undertone beneath his words still stung. 'No,' she said hastily. 'In fact, it's actually got better,' she lied.

There was a silence, and then Freddie said softly, 'That's great!' He paused. 'If it was true. But I know when you're lying, and you just lied to me. Which means it's a whole lot worse than you're letting on. Which leads me back to why I rang you in the first place—'

'To tell me I'm right to stay here,' Flora interrupted, resenting Freddie's hectoring tone and feeling a familiar wave of panic rise up.

'No! To tell you that I'm coming over to help—'

'Oh, no, you're not, Freddie. You are *not* coming!' Curling over the phone, she pushed her coffee cup across the table with a shaking hand. 'I do not need you to fight my battles.'

'So you admit you're fighting with him?'

Flora breathed out slowly. 'Please, Freddie. Don't cross-examine me. I'm fine. I don't need your help.'

'Spartacus had help. And he still lost.'

She winced. Her nails were cutting into her hand. 'He had to fight the entire Roman Army,' she said breathlessly. 'I just need to stay put. Keep my head down. Like you said. Besides, I think we've reached a sort of understanding.'

'Meaning what?'

Colour touched her brow and cheeks. Meaning that she'd kissed a man she should despise. Not a peck on the cheek but a passionate, feverish kiss that even now sent scalding heat across her skin.

There was silence, and then in the background she heard a phone begin to ring.

'Damn it! Look, I have to take this call—but do me a favour, Flossie. Think about what you're doing and then maybe you can try and explain to me why you're putting yourself through all this—because I really don't understand what you think you're achieving.'

With relief, Flora hung up. She was never a match for her brother in full 'gown and wig' mode, but trying to explain her actions to him would be impossible—mainly because she had no idea how to explain them to herself.

Heart racing, she lifted her bag to find her purse—and then her blood suddenly seemed to stop moving as she caught a glimpse of a familiar face, gazing out at her from between the headlines. Slowly, with a hand that shook slightly, she picked up the newspaper and gazed at Massimo Sforza's unmistakable profile.

Except it wasn't *his* face that caused her to raise her hand in front of her eyes. It was the face of the woman he was kissing. His *fiancée*.

Her eyes barely moved as she read the story, but her thoughts were writhing. He was *engaged*! She felt a rush of blood to her head. He was despicable. Revolting. And faithless. She shivered.

'Your bedroom or mine?'

He'd actually asked her that! Worse, for one infinitesimal moment she'd actually given it some consideration.

She glanced circumspectly around the café, half expecting to see people pointing and staring at her, but everyone was chatting and eating quite normally. Folding the newspaper, she called the waiter over and ordered another coffee.

She felt dreadful. She had kissed a man who was about to get married. That poor woman! This was exactly why she liked being single. So what if she didn't have a date on Valentine's Day? At least there were no nasty surprises. No disappointments. No pain.

Laying down the paper, she nodded automatically as the waiter placed the coffee in front of her. And then she glared at the photograph of Massimo and quickly covered his cheating, unscrupulous features with the cup. A shadow fell across the table

'Sugar?'

It was the waiter again. Pinning a weak smile onto her face, she looked up and shook her head. 'No, thank you. I don't—'

Her words died on her lips and her smile dropped from her face. Wearing a pale pink shirt that seemed only to accentuate his flagrant masculinity, Massimo Sforza was gazing down at her, his impossibly handsome face perhaps the cruellest reminder she'd ever had that beauty truly was skin-deep.

'You don't what?' He slid into the empty seat beside her as waiters from either side of the café converged on their table like a pack of eager dogs waiting for a bone. Barely turning round, he rattled off his order and settled back in his chair, his blue eyes never leaving her face. 'What is it that you don't do?'

Ignoring his question, she sat up stiffly. 'I don't know what you're doing here or how you found me,' she croaked, 'but I don't remember inviting you to join me so perhaps you'd like to leave.'

He frowned. 'Really? That's not very friendly. You were a lot friendlier yesterday.'

His eyes gleamed maliciously, and she gripped her cup tightly. Her hand was aching with the effort of not throwing her coffee all over his infuriating face, but losing her temper in front of so many witnesses would not be a smart move. Especially as they were probably all plain clothes police officers on Massimo's payroll.

'Was I?' she said, forcing herself to lift her chin and meet his glinting gaze. 'It happens sometimes…'

He shook his head slowly, a cold smile tugging at his lips. 'So that's how you want to play it, is it? *Grazie!*'

Flora blinked as he nodded curtly to the waiter who had appeared at his side to deposit an espresso and a glass of iced water onto the table.

'I suppose I should be grateful you aren't pretending to have amnesia.'

She glowered at him. 'Is that what you do, then?' she said stiffly. 'When you're with your *fiancée*?'

He picked up his cup of coffee and drank it swiftly. 'Absolutely,' he said coolly. 'As I have no memory of actually having a fiancée.'

Their eyes met—hers furious, his a clear, challenging blue.

'Really? Does she know that?' Gritting her teeth, Flora breathed out slowly. 'I'm surprised you even feel the need to pretend. That would imply guilt, and you don't feel guilt, do you? Feelings are just for little people. The sort of people you trample over to get what you want. Because that's all that matters, isn't it? Getting what you want.'

He stared straight at her, his gaze so focused that she felt as though her skin was melting, and then, leaning forward, he gently tugged the newspaper out from under her cup and unfolded it.

'*Now* I understand,' he murmured softly.

He looked up at her, his expression relaxed and composed, and yet she knew he was watching her closely.

She scowled at him. 'I doubt that. You and I are at opposite ends of the spectrum.'

Her heart thudded against her chest as his eyes met hers. 'And opposites attract!'

CHAPTER FIVE

THERE WAS A pulsing silence. Flora stared at him, imprisoned by the dark, lambent heat in his gaze, and then he smiled—a lazy, knowing smile that made her whole body shiver.

'You really shouldn't believe everything you read in the papers, you know,' he said softly. 'Although naturally I'm flattered that you find me so interesting.'

Her face flared with anger and embarrassment. 'I do *not* find you interesting!' Reaching out, she tried to snatch the paper away from him, but he fended her off easily.

'No, no, *no*! I don't normally read this drivel, but since you were so kind as to buy a copy...'

'I did *not* buy it,' she said shrilly. 'Someone left it on the table!'

'Of course they did,' he murmured, his pacifying tone clearly designed to provoke more than placate. 'Now, let's see what I've been up to!'

Flora sat back in her chair, gritting her teeth as his eyes skimmed over the newsprint.

Finally, he looked up at her and shrugged.

'Is that it?' she snapped. 'That's all you've got to say?'

He frowned. 'I'm a public figure. Being in the gossip pages goes with the territory.'

She gave him an icy glare. 'I'm not talking about the

ethics of journalism. I'm talking about the fact that you're engaged to be married!'

Amusement flickered across his face. 'You want facts? Okay. I'm not engaged, so naturally there will be no summer wedding.' He rolled his eyes. 'Nor did I date her sister or her stepmother.' The corners of his mouth twitched. 'And I'm absolutely *not* going to expand into shipping. Which is fortunate as it sounds quite painful, don't you think?'

Flora swallowed. It would be so easy to smile back at him. He was so ridiculously handsome, with his tanned skin, jay's wing eyes and sleek dark hair—all gold and blue and black, like a portrait of some medieval prince.

But that curving smile was as dangerous and deceptive as any hairpin bend, and curling her fingers into her palms to stop herself from grinning back at him, she scowled. 'Okay. So she's not your fiancée,' she said stubbornly. 'But she's still your girlfriend.'

Massimo took a mouthful of coffee and frowned. 'Alessa? No. She's just—easy!' He met her eyes and shook his head impatiently. 'Not *that* kind of easy. I mean she's uncomplicated. She's single and fun. She doesn't have an agenda and she's photogenic. A dream date! At least according to my public relations team.'

Flora stared at him incredulously. 'Her name is *Allegra*.'

His face didn't change, but she saw something glitter in his eyes. 'Whatever. She comes to any name.'

She felt her face drain of colour. 'You're disgusting.'

His face hardened. 'I thought you wanted facts?'

She shook her head. 'I don't want anything from you.'

Massimo watched her closely. She was lying. Her body was betraying her. She wanted him. Just as he wanted her. Or she had done until he'd made that stupid crude remark.

Watching the tension on her face, he shifted in his chair. 'I'm sorry. That was a cheap thing to say.'

She turned towards him, her face flushed. 'Yes, it was.'

Her eyes met his, and he saw the green flecks dancing angrily in their tawny depths.

'Why would you talk about somebody like that? If you think that little of her, why are you even seeing her?'

A sharp, nameless pang shot through him. Why, indeed?

He pushed the thought away and stared past her at the crowd of mid-morning shoppers. 'That's precisely why I am seeing her, *cara*,' he said lightly.

'That doesn't make any sense!'

He saw the confusion in her eyes, could hear it in her voice. But how could he explain how he felt? That caring—truly caring for someone—was never going to be part of his life. Not now. Not in the future. His past had made sure of that. Even now, just thinking about it made him feel sick to his stomach. Just like when he was a child—

An all-too-clear memory of pleading down the phone at boarding school, begging his father to let him come home for the holidays made it suddenly hard for him to breathe.

For a moment, he stared fixedly at the empty coffee cup, waiting for his body to forget what his mind couldn't. Finally, he forced himself to meet her gaze. 'It makes perfect sense. Think of a relationship as a bank account. If you have one with a lower rate of interest, you're not going invest much money in it, are you?'

Shaking her head, her eyes flashed angrily. 'And that's what this woman is to you? A low-interest account? Wouldn't it be more satisfying to actually be with someone you *do* want to "invest" in?'

She was chewing her lower lip and he felt his body grow hard, remembering how that soft pink mouth had surrendered to his hungry kisses. 'It's sweet of you to worry about me,' he said slowly, 'but I promise you I get regular dividends.'

There was a slow, pulsing silence as he watched the colour rise over her throat and cheeks, and then she lifted her chin, her eyes challenging him. 'Oh, I'm not worried about you—I'm sure your relationships suit your *unique* personality perfectly.'

He burst out laughing. She was such an odd mix: stubborn and scrappy as one of those cats that roamed the Coliseum; yet teasing and tempting him with her soft eyes and sweet smile.

A tension he hadn't acknowledged before eased inside him. It was strange: normally he found it difficult—more like impossible—to talk about something as personal as relationships. Talking meant thinking, and thinking meant feeling, and feelings were like a summer sea: tranquil on the surface but underneath swarming with riptides and jagged rocks.

Only it didn't feel like that talking here, now, with Flora. Instead, he felt as though she'd walked into his life, throwing open all the windows and ripping the dust sheets off the furniture. And instead of exposed, he felt exhilarated—excited, even.

'You know, you're wasted stuck out in the gardens talking to flowers. You should go into politics. Or maybe you could come and work for me in my public relations department.'

Her fingers twitched. 'What? So you can boss me about at work as well as in my own home? I think not!'

'You think I bully my staff?'

'I think you bully anyone and everyone!' she said bitterly. 'Whatever it takes to get your own way. You were probably in nappies the last time you actually had to do something you didn't want to do!'

Around him, the noise of the café seemed to retreat like a drawn breath, and despite the heat of the midday sun, he shivered as her words pressed against the black bruise of the past.

'Actually, it was more recent than that.' His voice sounded wrong—flat and tired—and he felt the air shift around them.

Her head snapped up. 'What does that mean?'

A thread of anger fluttered inside him, and he grabbed it gratefully. 'It means that you're going off-topic,' he said coldly. 'I'm not here to discuss my character or even yours. Unless it's somehow relevant to what happened yesterday.'

Leaning backwards, he gestured lazily for another glass of water.

There was another long silence. He watched her face grow still and furtive and felt a sharp jolt of satisfaction. *Let her sweat!* She'd been so determined to chastise him about his supposed engagement that she'd forgotten all about their own little assignation in the garden. Unfortunately for her, he hadn't. And after that grilling she'd just given him he wasn't about to let her wriggle off the hook.

His gaze rested on her face until finally, scowling, she met his eyes. 'Fine! Look… It was wrong. *I* was wrong. I don't know why it happened, but it won't happen again—'

Reaching out, he picked up a piece of ice from the glass of water and sucked it between his lips. 'How do you know?' he said lazily.

She stared at him blankly. 'I— What?'

'How do you know it won't happen again if you don't know why it happened?' He studied her face, enjoying her discomfort.

Flora gritted her teeth. She could no longer deny that she wanted him. How could she when she could feel the beat of desire throbbing in her veins? But sleeping with

Massimo...even the idea of it set off alarm bells inside her head.

Her mouth was dry. More than anything, she wanted to flee—not just from the undercurrents of tension swirling between them but the intensity of her response to him. Only despite knowing she should run like hell from his compelling, disturbing presences, something vague, some wavering thread kept tugging them closer.

Only being closer scared her more than the thought of having sex with him. Her heart gave a leap as though it too wanted to escape. If only she could crawl under the table and hide. But she could tell simply by looking at the set of his jaw that running away would only prolong her agony.

'I don't,' she said flatly.

He frowned. 'So it could happen again? That's a little worrying, don't you think?' The corners of his mouth twitched. 'I mean, what if you lose control and try and take advantage of me?'

She lifted her face to his and he saw the fear and the longing in her eyes, and in the shake of her head, and the fluttering pulse at the base of her throat. She wanted him. But she was going to fight him every inch of the way. The thought both exasperated and excited him unbearably.

Licking her lips, she stared at him confusedly. The sudden shift of his mood from tormenting to teasing made her insides lurch. And then slowly he smiled, his blue eyes flickering over her skin like a naked flame, cutting off her breath in her throat.

Around her the pastel-coloured stuccoed buildings began to waver in the sunlight. Desperately, she clutched the table like a lifebelt, and then her heart gave a quivering lurch as he reached over and took her hand.

'Why don't we stop this, *cara*? We're both adults. And we both want the same thing. So let's stop playing games—'

His hand was warm and light on hers. His thumb moving gently, caressing her skin like a warm tide.

Her head was spinning. It would be so easy to surrender to the golden glow of his touch. Taking a small, shallow breath, she glanced helplessly around the cafe. An
elderly man and his wife were smiling at her, their lined
faces soft with approval. No doubt they thought she and
Massimo were some young couple—a pair of newlyweds,
maybe. She breathed out sharply. Whatever they thought
they were seeing, they were wrong. And she must have
absolutely no sense of self-preservation if she was going
to let that beautiful, lethal smile blind her to the perils of
getting involved with him any more than she already had.

For where would that involvement end? Probably he
would grow bored with her the minute she surrendered
her body to his. And that would be humiliating. But hu-
miliation was the *most* positive outcome here. What would
happen if she fell in love? Her stomach twisted. A memory
of her father slid into her head: hunched, shrunken on a
sofa, clutching her mother's cardigan, his face wet with
tears. Her face tightened. Then her pain would be infinitesimal and immutable.

She shivered.

Love! She'd read the poems and listened to the songs on
the radio. But love wasn't just about devotion or even passion. It was about sacrifice too. And if you had that sort of
love—a love that exploded inside you and sent shock waves
to the tips of your fingers—then at some point you would
end up paying. And it would take everything you had.
Your strength, your health, your happiness, your sanity.

She bit her lip and abruptly withdrew her hand from his.
'You're right. We do want the same thing. But the difference between us is that I know that's not enough of a rea-

son to have sex.' She spoke quickly, her desire to be gone giving force to her words.

Beckoning for the waiter, she pushed back her chair and threw a handful of coins onto the table.

His face hardened. 'Why are you fighting this?'

'Because it's *wrong*,' she shot back. 'Wrong. And stupid.'

'You didn't think that yesterday!'

His voice was filled with frustration, but it was the chill in his eyes that whipped the breath from her throat.

'That was then—' she said hotly.

'Oh, please!' His scorn, sharp-edged, sliced through her denial. 'If I kissed you now you'd kiss me right back.'

The truth felt like a blast of cold air. She took a deep breath. Why *was* she fighting it? Would it really matter if she took his arm and led him to some anonymous hotel in the town? For a moment, she could almost feel the weight of the door key in her hand. Could feel the shimmering heat between their naked bodies—

She straightened her shoulders. Sex made everything *seem* so simple. All it required was some bodies and the right mix of hormones. But no matter how much she ached to feel the weight of his body on hers she wasn't going to give in. No amount of ecstasy was worth risking the pain and loss her father felt.

She breathed out slowly as, behind her, a bus pulled noisily into the square. 'Yes. I kissed you,' she said defiantly. 'And I'm not going to pretend I didn't enjoy it or that I don't find you attractive. Only it's not enough. Not enough for me to sleep with you. It might have been if we felt the same way. But we both know your motives have nothing to do with passion and everything to do with paying me back for getting in your way.'

Massimo stared at her, caught between anger and admiration. She was right to question his motives although she was also wrong: he *didn't* want to pay her back. Maybe at first he'd simply intended to exploit their powerful sexual attraction and thereby make her more malleable. But now his motives seemed to be growing more complex and confused. Just as the ache in his groin grew ever more intense and painful.

Watching his face harden, she felt her heart beat high in her throat—and then the tension seemed to drop inside her. Suddenly, for the first time in days, she felt calm. Wanting sex for its own sake wasn't wrong. But she knew deep down that Massimo's desire for her was motivated more by power than lust. Her refusal to move out had simply fuelled his desire to have his own way: if he couldn't have the *palazzo* he would have her instead. And that was wrong.

Her heart was thumping painfully hard and, feeling almost light-headed, she came to a sudden decision.

'Like I said, it's not a reason to stay but it *is* a reason for me to move out.' Snatching her handbag from the table, she stood up abruptly. 'I'll send someone to pick up my stuff. Congratulations. You've got what you wanted!'

She heard Massimo swear softly, saw his hand reach out to stop her, and then she turned and darted across the pavement towards the bus, slipping between the doors as it started to rumble away from the square.

Switching off the shower, Flora wrapped herself up in the towel provided by the *pensione* and stared glumly at herself in the small chipped mirror above the sink. Last night she'd been on a high, but now things felt slightly different. Her elation had dissipated, leaving behind the miserable realisation that, while she might have succeeded in having the last word, she had made herself homeless in the process.

She sat down on the bed and watched the cafés in the street below set up their tables.

So what was she going to do now? She couldn't stay holed up in the *pensione* for ever. Sooner or later she would have to go back to the *palazzo* to pack. And then it hit her. She hadn't just made herself homeless: her seedlings and plants, including her precious night-flowering orchids, would soon be on the streets too.

She bit her lip. Unless Massimo would agree to let them stay in the greenhouses. But it seemed unlikely. He would probably just laugh in her face. Tears pricked her eyes and she angrily swatted them away and took a deep breath. Tonight. She would go tonight and collect her orchids and leave the rest of her life behind. Start again. Live light. It would be an adventure. Besides, much as she loved the *palazzo*, the thought of being responsible for it had always made her feel edgy and uptight.

Feeling a little happier, she began to dry her hair.

Incredibly, she'd managed to hitch a ride most of the way to the *palazzo*, but it was still nearly nine before she finally slipped through the side door. The house was dark and strangely silent in a way that it hadn't been for weeks and she sighed with relief.

He was out! Probably celebrating her departure. But at least it meant she wouldn't have to see his stupid, smug face.

Feeling her way around the furniture, she made her way carefully through the house until finally she saw a glimmer of light. Her first thought was that at least she wouldn't break her neck on the stairs, but then, as she stepped into the hallway, something like fear scraped over her skin.

The front door was wide open and moonlight was shining straight through the doorway into the hallway. On legs that felt as though they were made of glass she walked softly across the floor. Looking nervously out into the darkness, her heart stopped as her thoughts tumbled into one another.

Massimo's car was still parked on the gravel beside the limousine. So he *was* home. Unless he'd taken a taxi. But then if he wasn't home why had he left the front door open?

She turned round and stared into the darkened house. And then the air seemed to shrink in on her as, with a sudden, paralysing lurch of fear, she heard something or someone move tentatively in the stillness. She froze, her stomach slowly turning to ice. But it was no good pretending she hadn't heard it. Somebody was inside the *palazzo*. Somebody who didn't want to be seen.

For a moment her body was rooted to the floor, her breath coming in panicky little gasps, and then there was a crashing sound, a muttered curse, and it was as though a pin had been pulled inside her. Anger, bright and blinding white, rose up and blossomed like a flare.

How dare they?

Gritting her teeth, she thought longingly of Umberto's ancient shotgun. It was broken and unloaded, but it still looked pretty damn scary. Only it was locked up in one of the outhouses. And then suddenly she saw the broom... leaning against the banisters, gleaming in the moonlight like some magical mythological weapon. Breathing out slowly, she picked it up and walked swiftly across the hallway and kicked open the kitchen door.

She had barely stepped into the room when she felt hands grab her. Strong male hands, gripping her round the waist and neck, twisting and crushing her. She lashed out with her feet and arms but her attacker was stronger, much stronger than she had ever imagined, and in sheer animal terror she sank her teeth into his arm.

'Let me go!'

He swore and, feeling his grip loosen, she yanked herself free. There was a cracking sound, and she staggered backwards with a cry.

'F-Flora?'

Her heart was crashing against her ribs so loudly that for a moment she wasn't sure if she was hearing things, and then she heard him curse softly in the darkness. Breathing out, she reached behind her and flicked on the lights, squinting as brightness filled the room.

'M-Massimo! What on—?'

He was suddenly beside her, his hands gripping her arms, his eyes the exact colour of a stormy night sky. 'You damned little fool! What the hell do you think you're doing, creeping around in the dark in the middle of the night? I could have broken your neck!'

Through the beating of her heart Flora could hear the shock in his voice. But she didn't care. A fury wilder than any storm reared up inside, splitting her open.

Tearing free of his grip, she thumped him hard in the chest. 'What do you mean? *You're* the one creeping around in the darkness. And how dare you tell me what I can and cannot do?'

Tension was shimmering off him like a heat haze. 'What *is* it with you? Don't you ever get tired of fighting me? It's like you're on some kind of mission!'

She glared at him, her eyes wide with disbelief. 'You *attacked* me!'

He stared at her incredulously. 'Then how come I'm the one bleeding?'

'You were hurting me!'

They were inches apart. She could feel the heat of his

body. He smelt of salt and leather, and despite her anger she felt heat spike up inside her.

He held up his hand. 'You bit me!'

'Good!' she snapped. 'It's the least you deserve after how you've treated me.'

'How I—' He stepped towards her, and she heard his sharply drawn breath. 'If you were a man—'

Her eyes narrowed. 'I'd wipe the floor with you.'

Her hands formed fists, but he was too quick for her. Grabbing her wrists, he pulled her against him. 'That's enough! Stop acting like a wildcat or—'

She tried yanking herself free, but he clamped her body closer.

They stared at each other, the tension pressing down on their skin, the air tightening around them.

'Or what?' she said hoarsely. 'You can't—'

'Oh, but I can,' he snarled and, lowering his head, he covered her mouth with his, stifling her protest with a kiss that tasted of fire and danger.

He pulled her closer, hard and fast, his body pressing against hers so that she could feel the thickness of his arousal. His mouth was hot, his tongue probing fiercely between her lips, teeth nipping, tugging, her body tingling, growing tighter and tighter—

Her breath shuddered, jerking out of her with a gasp as his fingers slid over her collarbone and over the thin fabric of her bra. She wanted him. More than she had ever wanted any man. His touch was like fire on her skin, melting her from the outside in. She shivered. Pleasure, like sunlight falling on leaves, swept over her. Her body burned with need. Her heart was racing…wild, frantic—

And then, like a drum beating out a warning rhythm, she heard the kitchen clock chime the hour and it saved her.

'No—' She broke away from him, stepping back clumsily.

'What—?'

He didn't move, but she saw something flicker in his eyes, only her brain seemed to be spinning on its own axis and she could barely speak, let alone make sense of his body language. 'No. We're not doing this. I told you.'

He was angry: his breathing unsteady, his gaze hostile and frustrated. 'Then why the hell did you come back?'

She blinked. Why *had* she come back? The question seemed to slip away from her, like a coin in a penny fall machine. Slowly, her thoughts began to level out and she met his eyes squarely. 'To get my orchids.'

He stared at her, his jaw tightening.

Catching the disbelief in his expression, she lifted her chin. 'They're *bulbophyllum nocturnum,*' she said defensively. 'Night-blooming orchids. They're very rare. It took me almost a year to convince Professor de Korver to send me some seeds.'

He frowned. 'Are they dangerous?'

She gaped at him. 'No! Why would they be dangerous?'

There was a short, tense silence and then he shrugged. 'I thought maybe you might be raising an army of ninja orchids. All armed with brooms, primed to attack me.'

Flora swallowed. He was teasing her, trying to lighten the mood. She wasn't ready for that but despite his earlier accusation, she was tired of fighting him. She shook her head.

'They're actually pretty ordinary, really, except they only flower at night. Usually I check in on them about eleven o'clock.'

'Do you tuck them up as well?' he said coolly.

Their eyes met and she bit her lip. 'I just want to collect them and then I'll leave,' she said stiffly.

A muscle flickered in his cheek. 'Then I'll *just* get my jacket.'

She stared at him in horror. 'I don't need an escort. I know my way—'

'And I need to know where you are. So. Either I go with you or you leave without your precious orchids.'

They walked in silence through the gardens, Flora stalking ahead like an angry cat.

Despite the almost tropical heat of the greenhouse she shivered in the darkness. It had been bad enough being alone with Massimo in the brightly lit kitchen. Now, in the sultry, sticky warmth of the greenhouses, with the leaves brushing against her face, it felt as if he was some big predator, stalking her through the jungle.

Holding a torch in one hand, she made her way carefully through the foliage. Behind her there was a muttered cursing as he banged into a watering can.

Turning, she frowned and said tersely, 'Be careful! You'll break something.'

'Yes. Like my neck,' he said irritably. 'Is that why you brought me out here? To finish me off?'

'Don't blame me! It was your idea to co—'

Abruptly, she stopped. 'Oh! I don't believe it! It's flowering. It's actually *flowering*!'

Massimo leaned round her and stared, bemused, at a small yellowish-green plant. 'It is?'

She nodded happily. 'I know it doesn't look like much but it's such an incredible plant. It's so stubborn, so determined to survive. And it's unique. There's no other orchid even remotely like it.' She let out a sigh of contentment. 'I can't believe it. I'm just so happy.'

Massimo stared at her in silence. The air around them tasted warm and perfumed, and something in her unguarded enthusiasm touched him. His heart was speeding and he took a step closer, his arm brushing against hers. 'So… Is that it, then?' he said hoarsely. He paused, his words jamming in his throat. 'Do you want to take them and go, or—?'

She looked up at him. His eyes looked almost black in the torchlight, the shadows making his face look younger, more vulnerable. She felt her stomach swoop down, as though she'd stepped off a diving board. Her breath was twisting in her throat. She should run. Or bite him again. Or maybe hit herself with the torch. Anything to stop this soft, gauzy heat creeping over her skin. She needed to focus, to concentrate on the facts. He was the enemy. Worse, he was an enemy who had managed to tear through all her carefully built up layers of logic and reason as though they were tissue paper.

But then what were they really but memories of her father's grief? Maybe now was the time to lay those ghosts to rest. After all, Massimo wasn't the love of her life: and this was only ever going to be sex.

Looking up, she saw the night sky, blue-black like a bruise, and suddenly she wanted to dive into it and lose herself beneath the inky surface. 'Or what…?' Her voice was husky, slipping and sliding with fear and longing.

'Or this…' he murmured softly, and slowly he lowered his head and kissed her.

It was a different kind of kiss. Softer. Slower. Sweeter. His pulse jumped as her lips parted, and he felt his groin tighten painfully. Groaning, he pulled her closer, his hands curling around her waist so that she was pressed against the full length of his arousal. Tearing his lips from her mouth, he kissed her neck, licking and nipping the petal-soft skin. He could feel her fingers tangling urgently through his hair, feel her breath coming in shuddering gasps as she dragged him closer.

'Massimo—'

His body stiffened even as his brain seemed to melt. Hearing her say his name was like a spike of adrenaline in his heart. He felt light-headed.

And then, moaning softly, she jerked away from him. 'Not here—'

They ran, stumbling, through the empty gardens and into the kitchen.

'Where do you want to—?' he began, but she stepped towards him, eyes blazing, and he reached out for her and jerked her into his arms, crushed her mouth against his.

She kissed him back, her lips parting as, breathing unsteadily, he nudged his knee between her legs, pushing her back against the table. His hands framing her face, he kissed her again and again with an urgency he'd never felt before. She tasted clean and cool—of springtime and green woods. His lips moved lower, kissing her neck, her throat, licking the salt from her skin. Hunger jack-knifed in his stomach as he heard her breath catch, felt her pulse flutter.

Flora felt her body tense as his hand slid under her T-shirt, her muscles spasming, a tingling heat swamping her. Her breath shuddered in her throat and desire…warm, sweet, liquid…rose up inside her as he moved between her thighs, flattening her body against his.

She shifted against him, frantic to soothe the sting of heat in her pelvis, and then she gasped as he tugged her dress down over her shoulders, down to her waist, and a sudden rush of cool air hit her overheated skin. Gripping the hard muscles of his arms, she shuddered as his fingers slid over her breasts, stroking and caressing her nipples, and then she moaned softly as she felt his lip curl around the rigid tip, grazing the soft dimpled flesh with his teeth.

She could feel the beat of his blood, pulsing over her skin, beating in time to her snatched breaths; her skin was prickling...pinpricks of fire threading out in every direction. Suddenly she wanted more and, body arching, she squirmed against him, frantically yanking at his belt—

Grunting, he reached down and tugged his trousers over his hips, then tore her panties down. His hand slid between her legs and she pressed against it. Heat was building inside her, dissolving and sparking into silver and white and a thousand kinds of gold.

'Touch me...'

She slid her fingers over the soft skin of his belly and then lower, over the cluster of dark curls, then lower still, until he groaned softly and grasped her head in his hands as a knife-sharp spasm of pleasure shuddered through his body.

As she locked her arms around his neck he shifted her weight and fumbled in his pocket. Reaching down, she took the condom and with hands that shook slightly, stroked it over the hard length of him. Hands reaching under to cup her buttocks, he lifted her in one strong movement, up and onto the table, and then he thrust into her so that she grabbed his shoulders, her nails digging into the smooth flesh.

With each thrust of his hips he drove into her deeper and harder, and she moved against him, rocking her hips faster and faster, until her body shuddered and, closing her eyes, she gripped him tightly as he groaned again and tensed inside her.

For a moment they stayed there, spent and sated, arms around one another, their bodies juddering with the aftershocks of their passion. She felt his lips brush against her hair. His arms tightened around her and as he gently withdrew she buried her face against his shirt.

She didn't want to look at him—didn't want to see her mistake in the curl of his lip. Not for a little while anyway. Not while his hands were still caressing her and while she could still feel the warmth of his body and the soft beating of his heart.

He would move soon enough.

But he didn't. And finally she forced herself to look up at him again. He was watching her, his face calm and serious. For a moment he said nothing, and she tensed, fearing his hesitation. And then, tilting her face upwards, he lowered his mouth and kissed her.

'Let's go to bed,' he said slowly. 'Together.'

And, reaching down, he scooped her into his arms and strode out of the kitchen and up the stairs.

Later, still shaken by the intensity of what they'd shared, she lay in his arms, watching him sleep. She felt stunned and sated and happy. Not that anything had changed really, she told herself carefully. They had simply had sex. And no matter how warm and safe, how tender she might feel right now, he was still as ruthless and single-minded as ever—just as a tiger in a zoo was as dangerous as a tiger in the jungle.

His arm was resting across her stomach and carefully, so as not to wake him, she rolled towards him to watch the play of dappled light across his lean chest. It didn't feel real, him being there. It was like a dream.

But what would happen when he woke up?

She tensed, fear scraping over her skin. And then, beside her, Massimo shifted in his sleep, his hand tightening possessively over her hip, and her fear dropped away.

Feeling calmer, she curled her arm over his chest. And as her eyes drifted shut she wondered drowsily what exactly he'd been doing in the dark in the kitchen. But it was too late to answer that question, for the next moment, lulled by the heat of his body and the comforting sounds of morning birdsong, she had fallen swiftly and deeply asleep.

CHAPTER SIX

MASSIMO BREATHED OUT SLOWLY.

Finally, she was asleep.

Staring up at the ceiling, he gritted his teeth and tried to work out exactly what was happening. It certainly wasn't what usually happened. Usually at this point he would have forgotten the woman's name—if he'd even known it at all—and, satiated by a night of passion, he would have been waiting for the earliest possible opportunity to leave.

And it should have been the same with Flora—in theory at least. Last night he'd taken her into his arms with the sole aim of working her out of his system—the same way he'd done time and time before with every other women he'd desired.

But from the start nothing had been straightforward with Flora. And now, at some point between last night and this morning, everything had changed again.

With her arm curled loosely around his body, it felt different between them. For a start he doubted he would ever forget her name...not after what had happened last night— he smiled tightly—and twice this morning.

His heartbeat shivered. His sex life was hardly vanilla. But Flora was the most erotic woman he'd ever known. Her feverish response to his touch had taken his breath away. She had been like fire and light in his hands, her body molten with heat. It had been incredible.

At the memory of just how incredible she'd been, he felt his body grow painfully hard and, shifting beneath the sheets, he frowned. What the hell was the matter with him?

So she was sexy... So what?

It wasn't as if there was a shortage of beautiful, eager women clamouring to share his bed. Flora was nothing special.

He gritted his teeth.

So why was he fighting an impulse to lean over and pull her closer? To press his lips softly against hers and wake her with a kiss? He'd never felt like that before. No matter how good the sex had been, he'd never once wanted to indulge in any sort of post-coital affection. He'd always wanted to break free, some deep-rooted need driving him on to the next one-night stand.

His heart banged painfully against his ribs. It didn't make any sense except— She wasn't just sexy, he admitted a moment later. She was beautiful.

And smart and determined.

And, unlike every other woman of his acquaintance, he lived with her.

Which was *clearly* the real reason he was still holding her in his arms. He felt a sudden swift stab of relief. Of *course*. It was obvious. Why would he drag himself out of one bed to get into another in the room next door?

Feeling calmer now that he'd rationalised his uncharacteristic behaviour, he turned his attention to more predictable matters: work! Swiftly, he clicked through his day's schedule. He had a conference call planned for just after ten, and then a lunch with an overseas investment bank.

He needed to prepare for both. But he was finding it impossible to concentrate on anything but Flora's warm body curving against his, her skin so smooth and soft and just begging to be touched.

He felt a rush of raw desire and, glancing down at her, his breath snagged in his throat. What was happening to him? It didn't make any sense.

Working…his job…the business he had built up from scratch had never taken second place to a woman before. Somewhere inside, something shifted and stirred, a shadow rising. He grimaced.

He knew what had happened. And when. It had been yesterday, in that café. For one tiny moment, he'd let Flora get under his skin. He never talked about personal matters but for some inexplicable reason, he'd let his guard down. *Hell!* He'd even hinted at his miserable childhood, he thought angrily. He let out a long, slow breath. Thankfully, though, he'd come to his senses before losing control completely and telling her the whole sordid story of his life.

His stomach tightened. He'd been close to blowing it all; dredging up feelings he'd buried in the furthest corners of his soul. He'd let lust and frustration impair his judgement.

But it wouldn't happen again. Flora might be sexy and beautiful, but she was dangerous too. Whenever he was with her—like yesterday—he didn't recognise himself. But whatever might have happened in that café, it didn't mean that he trusted her. His mouth twisted. Since his father's betrayal he hadn't been able to trust anyone, and he couldn't see that changing any time soon. Probably never. And he was glad. That way the pain of the past would stay in the past.

Beside him, Flora shifted in her sleep, moaning softly. Glancing down at her, he smiled grimly, his confusion forgotten. He'd been careless, that was all. Soon, she would join the long list of women with whom he'd shared a one-night stand. But before that happened, he wasn't about to

turn down what she was offering. After all, he was a normal red-blooded male with natural urges. So why argue
with nature?

And, gently lifting her arm, he shifted down the bed
and woke her with a kiss.

Much later, Flora woke again to the sound of running
water. The bed was empty and, stretching slowly, she wriggled free of the sheet and sat up. She could just see Massimo in the shower. His gorgeous male body was blurry
through the glass, but she felt a shiver of pleasure as she
remembered his golden skin and the hard muscles of his
chest and back.

For a moment she lay and watched him, her body
twitching at the memory of his dark touch, his strong,
firm hands drawing out her desire, smoothing her skin,
roaming over her body, so intimate, so possessive.

It had felt so *right*—the weight of his body on hers and
the way she'd moved and cried out and begged—

A blush swept over her skin and, closing her eyes, she
pressed her face against the cool cotton of the pillowcase.

Not that she was ashamed. It was just that she hadn't
known sex could feel like that. So wild and intense and
beautiful. It certainly hadn't ever been like that for her
before. Her cheeks grew warmer. The truth was, she had
barely recognised herself.

She'd been like a wild creature, driven by a fierce
hunger such as she had never known—a hunger that had
swamped her and pulled her under so that she had lost
herself in the darkness.

Rolling onto her back, she breathed out deeply. But
she had survived. Better than survived. She was fine. She
felt calm and happy. For the thing she had dreaded hadn't
happened.

She had feared that at some point her feelings would get tangled up in their feverish coupling. And that no matter what she did she would find herself ensnared: feeling, caring, loving.

She shivered.

But it hadn't happened. She might have surrendered to his touch, but she knew now that she would give nothing more. And why should she? Who needed feelings when they could have that fire of passion?

Her eyes were still closed when she realised that the shower had stopped—and then, almost before she had a chance to process the implications of that thought, she knew that Massimo was in the room. Her skin began to tingle and her stomach flipped over. Nerves humming, she opened her eyes.

He was watching her, leaning against the doorjamb with an easy animal grace that made her heart quiver. He was wearing nothing but a towel knotted round his waist, his bare chest still damp, the smooth lines of his muscles knife-sharp, like sculpted marble.

But it wasn't just his muscles that looked like stone. His face was lean and hard and unsmiling, and she suddenly realised two things: one, she was holding her breath, and two, in her haste to examine her own response to what had happened she had pretty much forgotten all about Massimo.

Her sense of calm started to drain away. It was easy telling herself that passion was enough. That she could choose when and what she should feel. But now, with his gaze pressing down on her skin, she realised that not only was that untrue, it was dangerously premature and presumptuous.

She waited, her nerves humming, but he seemed in no hurry to speak; he just studied her face with eyes that were the same cool blue as an Alpine sky.

Finally, when she was on the verge of screaming out loud, he said calmly, 'Did you sleep okay?'

His voice was cool too. It felt like shards of ice skittering over her skin. It was the voice of a stranger or an adversary. She stared at him, confused; after what they'd shared last night she'd been expecting some small degree of warmth. But then, given that up until last night they'd spent most of their time sparring with one another, perhaps this moment was never going to be anything but awkward.

She nodded warily. 'Yes. How about you?'

He nodded and there was a tiny, sharp silence, and then abruptly he held out his hand, and she felt a curl of happiness rise up like smoke inside her. He was offering her an olive branch. That meant everything was okay between them. That maybe last night had given him as much pleasure as it had given her.

Lifting her hand, she smiled up at him—and then her stomach seemed to go into freefall as, frowning, he pointed past her to the bedside table. 'Could you pass me my watch? I need to know what time it is.'

Her cheeks felt as if they were on fire. She felt stupid and small. But what had she really imagined would happen today? Last night might have left her breathless and dazzled. But to a man like Massimo—a man whose sexual escapades were splashed over the newspapers—it was clearly commonplace, and there was no point in getting upset about that quite obvious fact.

She lifted her chin, feeling her temper rise. Getting upset was at the bottom of her agenda. Her pride demanded that she stayed cool and unemotional—or that she appeared to do so at least. In fact, if she was going to survive this fling with any shred of her dignity intact she needed to remember this moment. Remember how it had made her feel.

She picked up the watch, glancing at it swiftly before

she handed it to him. 'Is that the time? I should get up,' she said briskly.

Rolling over, she slid out of the bed and pulled on her dress.

He watched her with that clear blue gaze that left scorch marks on her skin, and despite her anger and disappointment she felt a fluttering sensation low in her pelvis. She gritted her teeth. It was not fair that he should still have this effect on her. Far worse though was the thought that he should know it and instantly she met his gaze, determined to match him look for look.

He smiled then—a cool, curling smile of such arrogance and ownership that her hands curled into fists—and her breath felt suddenly hot and tight in her throat. Why was he looking at her like that when moments earlier he'd been acting as though he couldn't wait for her to be gone? No doubt it was some technique he'd picked up in business—some trick to intimidate a rival. Shape-shifting so that it was impossible to know what he would say or do next.

Looking up, she read the challenge in his gaze and felt her skin start to prickle.

Was it any wonder the sex had been so hot and fierce and wild? she thought shakily. It was just an extension of how they interacted outside of the bedroom: pushing boundaries, playing games; taunting one another. Every word, every touch, was just another move in their desperate power struggle.

She clenched her teeth. It was bad enough that this man had such a strong effect on her. Indecent, almost. But if she didn't make a stand then she would more or less be giving him carte blanche to walk all over her.

She took a deep breath. 'Actually, I should probably be going. I've got a load of notes to write up.'

She saw his eyes harden and felt a rush of satisfaction.

Now he knew how it felt when somebody blew hot and cold. The fact that she really did have loads of notes to write up was actually beside the point; she would happily have told him she needed to fly to Jupiter to collect rare orchid seeds if it meant she could leave his disturbing presence with her pride intact. Or at least with his a little dented.

His eyes narrowed. 'Really!' he said softly. She took a small step backwards, suddenly desperate to get some distance between them.

He was dangerous. And desirable. Or maybe they were the same thing. She didn't know any more. Didn't know anything except that she needed to go somewhere she wouldn't be tempted to reach out and touch him.

'Yes. And I'm sure you've got meetings and stuff,' she insisted, pressing her knees together in an effort to stop the teasing ache between her thighs.

He moved away from the door with a languid grace that made her insides melt and she inched backwards.

'Stuff?' he repeated. 'What kind of stuff?'

She looked at him blankly. Every atom of her body was straining with the effort of not turning and running away and her head seemed empty of thought. 'You know… Shouting and jack-booting around.' Her voice was tightening up, and nervously she watched his eyes flicker over her face.

'Shouting and jack-booting isn't until tomorrow,' he said quietly, taking a step towards her. 'Today I thought I'd work from home. Maybe brush up on disciplinary procedures.'

Her cheeks flooded with colour, her lips parting. She stared at him wordlessly, trying to think of something smart and flip to say, but she could hardly breathe much less think straight. Then suddenly she didn't care about being smart or cool. All she wanted was to get out of the room before he demolished all her self-control and reason.

She took a deep breath. 'Look, I know there's probably some slick way of asking this, but I don't know how to do it. So I'm just going to ask you straight. What are we doing here? I mean, was this it? Or do you want to sleep with me again?'

Massimo studied her face in silence. Her words seemed to hover and hum in the air between them, and he almost reached up to brush them away. He hadn't expected her to act like this. Although, truthfully, he'd hardly given any thought at all to how she would react to what had happened between them.

Probably he would have imagined her just as she had been a moment ago, lips parted, cheeks flushed. No fear: just fire. But this was different. *She* was different. Her eyes were wide and clear. Not challenging, just grave and real.

He knew those eyes. Knew what they were asking. Knew too how hard it was to ask. It had had taken a lot of guts.

The silence stretched out between them, dissolving and blurring into the silences of his childhood. How many times had he waited, his heart in his throat, for answers to questions he'd had no choice but to ask? For a moment he was lost, alone in the past, and then her face slid into focus and breathed out slowly.

'I want you and I know you want me too,' he said bluntly. Her lashes flickered up and she met his gaze, her face wary but with a flicker of curiosity in her eyes. 'Besides, that was the best sex I've ever had.'

He smiled at her slowly and Flora felt a shimmering pleasure unfurl inside her even as her heart contracted at his stark choice of words. She nodded slowly. 'Okay, so let me get this clear. This is just sex.'

'That's right. Unless you fancy doing my laundry…?' he drawled.

He was teasing, and part of her wanted to be teased. But she needed to know. 'And it's just the two of us?'

It was supposed to be a statement, only it came out like a question and her nails bit into the palms of her hands as something flickered across his eyes. Slowly, he glanced down at her fists and then back to her face.

'I'm all yours,' he said softly. 'And you, *cara*, are all mine.'

His hand on her skin was warm and firm, and she gave a start of surprise as leaning forward, he slowly began to undo the buttons on her dress. His arm slid round her waist and he pulled her closer. 'And I'm not sharing you with anyone.'

Her head was spinning. Desperately, she tried to hang on to her self-control. She'd told him she had to leave and she should go. Another minute and she would be lost, all caution gone, her mind sliding away, claimed by the fierce pull of his gaze and the light, teasing touch of his fingers.

'I really should be going…' Her voice was husky and she couldn't keep the shake out of it.

He lifted his hand from her dress and stroked her face, his fingers light and tender, tracing the line of her cheekbone, brushing over her lips. And then, as she opened her mouth to repeat herself, he lowered his head and kissed her.

He tasted of mint and salt, and she felt her stomach tense as he parted her lips with his tongue and kissed her hungrily. She pressed against him as his hands travelled over her skin, pulling her against him so close that their bodies felt as one. His breathing was raw, almost savage against her throat, his pulse jerking with hers as he licked and kissed the skin of her neck.

She bit into his shoulder as his fingers curved under the

swell of her buttocks, firm and sure, their touch so precise and so in control. Every touch, every breath was changing her. The room was growing lighter and lighter in time with the tantalising beat pulsing through her body.

And then from somewhere outside the window she heard the faint humming of a bee, and with an almighty effort she pulled away from him. 'No. Not now—'

His eyes narrowed. 'What are you talking about?' He glanced down at the thickness of his erection through the towel. 'Do you think I can put this on hold?'

She glared at him. 'I don't know. Anyway, why are you yelling at me? It was you who started it. You didn't have to kiss me.'

'I'm not yelling. And what was I supposed to do? You were waiting to be kissed—'

'I was not!' Her eyes flashed angrily. 'We were just talking. Getting things straight. I'd already told you I have work to do.'

'Work!' He blew out a long breath. 'I think it can probably wait, don't you?'

She glowered at him. 'You mean it's okay to put that on hold?'

He shook his head slowly, his eyes glittering. 'Why are we even having this conversation?'

She stared at him furiously, her cheeks flushed with anger. 'Because you didn't listen to me.'

His face twisted irritably. 'I didn't realise you were being serious.'

'No. What you meant was that you don't think my work is serious. Well, it is and I am. I actually do have work to do.' Not that it was really about that. She just wasn't about to let him walk all over her. 'Look... Maybe this wasn't such a good idea after all.' She bit her lip and glanced away.

He stared at her in silence.

Work aside, this was probably the longest conversation he'd ever had with a woman. Probably the *only* conversation he'd ever had with a woman. And he still wasn't exactly sure why he was having it. She wanted to have sex and so did he. That was what they'd agreed. His face tightened. Only now she was saying she had to work! And that their sleeping together wasn't a good idea.

Was she seriously going to choose her thesis over him? As if that compared to running a global company. Although truthfully neither his business nor even the *palazzo* project seemed as important as convincing her that this affair could work.

He gritted his teeth. Who the hell did she think she was? And what possible reason would he have to hang around while she *wrote up her notes*? Didn't she know how many women would be more than willing to satisfy his needs? But for some inexplicable reason he didn't want just *any* woman. He wanted this stubborn, maddening woman standing in front of him.

Abruptly, he held out his hand, frowning as she eyed it warily. 'It's okay. I'm not going to jump your bones.' Reluctantly, she took his hand and, curling his fingers around hers, he pulled her closer. 'You're right. And I'm sorry. I can wait…'

He breathed out slowly and drew away.

'Go on. Go and do your work.' His gaze locked onto hers. 'But only if you promise to let me take you out to lunch.'

He stared at her intently, watching the indecision in her eyes. He hated having to negotiate with her. It reminded him of his childhood. Of the fear and uncertainty of life with his father and stepmother. But let her play her games—let her think that this act of defiance would somehow change the balance of power between them. He'd soon show her exactly who was in charge.

She nodded slowly, her face softening. 'Okay. But you have to let me pay half. That way it won't feel like a date.'

She met his gaze, and he nodded, but as he watched her walk out through the door his smile faded. She might think she was going out to lunch in Cagliari, but a crowded restaurant was not the place for what he had in mind. He needed somewhere private—somewhere he could strip her naked and play a few games of his own.

In the meantime, though, he needed to take another shower. And the colder, the better.

Pushing the gearstick hard to the left, Massimo dropped down a gear and effortlessly steered the Lamborghini down the curving hillside. It was a beautiful day, with a clear delphinium-blue sky and a warm breeze. Glancing at Flora, he grinned as he saw the golden flecks in her eyes. She was enjoying herself.

As though reading his mind, she turned to him and gave him a smile of such sweetness that he almost crashed the car.

'It's incredible!'

He laughed. 'I like it—even though it is a bit of cliché!'

She frowned. 'Does that make me a cliché too?'

He laughed again. 'You definitely aren't a cliché, *cara*!' His eyes slid approvingly over her short green dress and bare legs. 'I like that colour on you. It brings out the green in your eyes.'

She smiled at him mischievously. 'It's called absinthe— after the drink.'

'Is that right?' He shook his head. 'So instead of fighting me, you're trying to drive me mad!'

Glancing at him sideways, she giggled. 'No. I thought it was an aphrodisiac.'

'Then *you* must be mad! An aphrodisiac is the last thing I need when I'm with you.'

Before he'd even thought about what he was doing, he reached over and gently rumpled her hair. He felt her arch her head beneath his hand, and as heat rushed through him, he slid his fingers over her collarbone, his thumb circling the pulse beating at the base of her throat.

'Maybe we could just go back to the *palazzo.*'

She heard the heat in his voice and, turning her head, she smiled. 'You're incorrigible. And I'm hungry and you promised me lunch. So keep your mind on the road and both hands on the wheel—otherwise you'll end up driving us both into a ditch.'

Ten minutes later they'd reached the outskirts of Cagliari.

'So where are we going?'

'I thought—' Massimo stopped. His phone had started ringing.

'Do you want to answer that?' she said quickly. 'I don't mind.'

He shook his head. Picking it up, he switched it to silent. 'It's not important. What did you ask me? Oh, yes. Where we're eating. I don't think you know it.'

Flora nodded. 'Oh. Okay. What kind of food is it?'

He shrugged. 'Seafood. Unless you don't like seafood?'

The change in him was so subtle that at first she thought she might have imagined it. But as he turned to check the oncoming traffic she saw that there was a slight tension in his shoulders, and the easy warmth in his eyes had been replaced by a dull anger. Not the raw antagonism that seemed to characterise their confrontations but a hard, icy, controlled fury that made a knot form in her stomach.

She stared at him uncertainly. 'I do. So, is it in the town centre?'

He nodded, and Flora frowned. 'But why are we at the marina then?'

She glanced past Massimo to where at least fifty huge yachts sat on the shimmering turquoise water, their gleaming white hulls like huge gulls.

He switched off the engine and turned to face her. 'Slight change of plan. But I know you'll love it.'

Sliding out of the car, he had walked round and opened her door before she'd even had a chance to open her lips.

'What do you mean, change of plan—?'

But he stifled her words with his mouth. Then, lifting his head, he gave her an irresistible grin and taking her hand firmly in his, began to walk towards the jetties.

'Where are we going?'

She was having to run to keep up with his long strides and suddenly she felt a little nervous. Everywhere she looked there were gorgeous women standing on decks, long legs gleaming in the sunlight, perfectly manicured hands resting on chrome rails that glittered almost as much as the jewels around their necks.

With horror, she realised that he was steering them towards one of the boats—the biggest, in fact—and she began to drag her feet.

'What is it?' He turned to face her, his handsome face creasing.

She hesitated. 'It's really very kind of you, but I can't just turn up at some party with a load of super rich, super loud, super confident friends of yours. It's just not my thing.'

He frowned. 'They're not really that rich. Or confident.' He tugged her gently towards the gangway. 'But they are super quiet. Listen.'

She listened, but all she could hear was the gentle slap of the waves against the side of the boat and the odd shrill cry of a gull. 'I can't hear anything.'

Gently, he rubbed at the worry lines between her eyes. 'That's because they don't exist.' He sighed. 'Why would I do that? Arrange an intimate lunch with you on my boat and then go and invite hundreds of guests along for the ride?'

She gaped at him. '*Your* boat? You *own* this?'

Something in her voice seemed to cut through the hard lump of tension inside him. For a moment back there, when his phone had started ringing, he'd almost changed his mind. But now, watching her eyes widen with astonishment, he felt calmer. Grinning, he tightened his grip on her hand and tugged her after him.

They were halfway up the gangway now and, looking up, Flora could see several men wearing shorts and T-shirts starting to assemble on the deck. 'Who are *they*?' she squeaked.

He glanced up. 'They're the crew.'

Crew! Flora felt her stomach flip over. But it was no good digging in her heels any more. They were on the boat now, and Massimo was shaking hands with the members of his crew.

Staring dazedly across the deck, she felt his hand around her waist and, taking a deep breath, she turned to face him. 'Isn't it a little small?' she murmured.

His eyes gleamed. 'It's eighty metres!'

She met his gaze, a smile tugging at her lips. 'So it's not true then, what they say about men with big boats…?'

He laughed softly.

She smiled up at him, and he felt his body grow hard at the soft, teasing look in her eyes. 'So, do I get to wear a uniform while I'm on the boat?'

'I don't know if we've got anything in your size,' he said, running his fingers along the bare flesh of her arm.

Inside his pocket he felt his phone vibrate, but today was going to be all about him and Flora. Nothing was going to come between them.

Probably not a uniform.

And certainly not his past.

CHAPTER SEVEN

'I CAN'T BELIEVE how soft this is. It feels just like powder.'

Reaching down, Flora picked up a handful of sand and let it run through her fingers. Her eyes narrowed thoughtfully as she glanced over her shoulder at the dunes that edged the beach.

'I wonder what grows here. Euphorbia, maybe? Anyway, it'll probably be something quite hardy—something that doesn't need many nutrients.'

Crouching down beside her, Massimo sighed. 'Probably,' he agreed. 'But I *do* need nutrients, *cara*. So can we please go and eat? Much as I love sand, you can't eat it— and I'm absolutely starving.'

He pulled her to her feet, and slowly they began to walk up the beach.

'Are you sure this is okay?' She looked up at him, not anxious, just curious. 'I thought you were going to work from home today?'

His gaze held hers. 'I'm the boss, *cara*. I make the rules. I don't follow them. Besides, today *is* about work.'

Her heart gave a thud. Of course—he'd probably brought her here to hassle her about the *palazzo*. She felt a sharp twist of anger. If only she hadn't allowed her stupid body to start calling the shots she might actually have seen that one coming.

'What do you mean?' she said dully.

His face was expressionless. 'One thing business has taught me is that you need to plan for the worst.'

'And what's that?' she croaked.

'I lose my job. My business. So, as I see it, spending time with you is just like training for a new career. If I can stop you from picking a fight with me, I reckon I could easily get a job as a diplomat. Give me a couple of weeks and I might even sort out peace in the Middle East—no problem.'

For a moment she couldn't breathe. She was too shocked... angry...relieved. Then, looking up at him, she saw that he was laughing. And after a moment she started to laugh too.

Massimo hesitated briefly and then took her hand in his. Her grip was firm, but not too tight, and it felt strangely relaxing walking beside her. It wasn't something he'd ever done before. He smiled grimly. Usually with a woman his hands were otherwise occupied. But he liked the way her fingers curled loosely around his.

He glanced at her sideways. She was such an intriguing mix of contradictions. One moment teasing him about bringing his wallet, the next bombarding him with questions about the boat. But he liked that too.

His mouth twisted.

Not that it really mattered either way. She was here because he wanted her here. It was a demonstration of his power, not some affirmation of her charms.

And, of course, it was a chance to enjoy the pleasures offered by that delectable body with no interruptions. Pushing his free hand into his pocket, something shifted inside him, as he felt the space where his phone should be.

'It's like paradise!'

Flora gazed happily at the clear blue water and the long, curving crescent of white sand and then turning to him, she frowned. 'But I don't understand why nobody else is here.'

He looked at her with amusement. 'Probably because it's private property!'

Catching sight of the confusion in her eyes, he grinned. 'Don't look so worried. I'm an old hand at trespassing. Remember?'

She felt a tingling warmth tiptoe over her skin. It was a good thing their relationship would only ever be about sex, she thought weakly. It would be perilously simple to start craving that curling smile; to start dreaming of ways to become the focus of that steady clear blue gaze.

She punched him lightly on the arm. 'I can't believe you brought me here. That's makes me some kind of accomplice!'

He gave her a long, slow smile. 'I wanted to see where your boundaries are—'

Transfixed by the many possible and all equally unsettling implications of his words, Flora decided it was definitely time to move the conversation on.

'So why is it so empty, then?' Unsettled by his glittering gaze, she spoke too quickly. For a moment, he simply stared at her so that she was holding her breath, her heart hammering in panic that he might have read her thoughts.

But after a long pause, he said coolly, 'Like I said. It's privately owned. Fortunately I happen to know the owner and he said we could stop off for lunch.'

She stared at him suspiciously. 'You're not the owner, are you?'

'One day, perhaps.' His expression was gently mocking. 'I might make him an offer when I'm ready to buy.'

He spoke calmly—as though he were discussing the possibility of buying a neighbour's car.

Suppressing a sigh, Flora nodded politely. Living

with him day to day, she'd been aware that Massimo was wealthy. But there was wealthy and then there was the sort of mind-boggling wealth that was quite impossible to picture. No wonder he'd been so furious when she'd refused to move out of the *palazzo*. If he could afford to buy an island, it must have come as a bit of shock when his money had failed to change her mind.

She felt another flicker of panic. Earlier, she'd felt strong and sure of herself. Despite wanting nothing more than to tumble back into bed with him, she'd forced him to see her not just as a conquest or a commodity but as a person. But now, transported by his luxury yacht to an exclusive piece of paradise she felt vulnerable and out of her depth—alone on an island with a man who not only didn't live in her world but clearly didn't expect to play by its rules either.

'You're very quiet.'

Massimo's voice broke into her thoughts.

'I was thinking.'

'I've got a cure for that.'

She felt his gaze sweep over her and, looking up, she found him watching her curiously. 'Thinking isn't a bad thing.'

He looked past her out to the open sea. 'Depends what you're thinking,' he said cryptically.

It was on the tip of her tongue to ask him what *he* was thinking. But just in time she remembered. This was just sex.

She didn't need to know what he was thinking and she certainly had no intention of sharing her thoughts. In truth, she'd rather die first.

She smiled up at him. 'Actually, I was just thinking that I would never have got to see the Spiaggia Rosa if you hadn't brought me out on your boat today.' She hesitated.

'So thank you.' She shook her head slowly. 'I still can't believe it's actually pink.'

He laughed. 'The clue's in the name.'

She rolled her eyes. 'I know it's called that. But lots of things have names that sound like one thing and then they turn out to be completely different. Like Leeds Castle,' she said triumphantly. 'Leeds is in Yorkshire but the castle's in Kent.'

There was short, taut silence, and then he said quietly, 'It was built next to a village in Kent which is also called Leeds. That's why it's called Leeds Castle.'

'How do you know *that*?' She stared at him in astonishment but he simply shrugged. For a moment she hesitated. This definitely had nothing whatsoever to do with sex but— 'Are you interested in castles, then?' she said tentatively.

His pace had slowed, and she sensed that he was deciding whether or not to tell her something. Finally, after several strides, he shook his head.

'I went to school in Kent. One year my class had to do a project on Leeds Castle.' His voice was flat and he was staring straight ahead. 'That's how I know so much about it. I don't actually remember much about the castle itself, except that it has a maze and a moat.' He smiled stiffly and let go of her hand. 'But then I was only seven, and seven-year-old boys find history pretty dull.'

Flora looked at him blankly. 'I didn't know your family lived in Kent. I thought you grew up in Italy. What were they doing in England?'

There was a stilted pause and then Massimo frowned. 'My family didn't live in Kent. I went to boarding school there. They were in Rome.'

His heart was beating slowly, like a funeral march. He gritted his teeth. What the hell was he doing? She didn't need to hear this stuff any more than he wanted to remember it. Except that saying it out loud, sharing it with Flora, made it feel different somehow.

He'd always thought that talking about it would bring back the pain. And it had. Only not in the way he'd imagined. It still hurt—how could it not? But this was not the dull, throbbing pain of loneliness and rejection. It felt more like the prickling ache that came when a wound was healing.

He felt her turn towards him and then saw her look away.

'Oh!' She swallowed. His words had shocked her, but it was the tension in his voice that made her flinch. 'Wow. That must have been quite hard for you. I mean, I still get homesick now and I'm twenty-seven. I can't imagine what it would have been like, going away from home when I was that young.'

He shrugged, holding up his hand almost defensively, as though to deter her sympathy.

'I didn't know any different. And it was actually a very useful life lesson. It taught me that you can only ever rely on yourself. That you don't actually need anyone in your life.'

Flora nodded. It was a brief, too brief glimpse into his mind and she badly wanted to ask him more. But the cool inflexibility of his voice was like a shutter coming down, and she knew that the topic was no longer up for discussion.

She smiled at him weakly, stunned and saddened. It might have been the slimmest of revelations but it went a long way to explaining the man he was. No wonder he was so detached and clinical. His parents hadn't just sent him away to school. They'd sent him to a different country. But they must have had some reason, she thought shakily. Only she knew that her own parents would never have made that choice.

'Fantastic. Lunch is ready!'

Massimo's voice bumped into her thoughts and, looking up, she felt her feet stutter to a halt.

Across the sand a huge canvas canopy was rippling gently in the breeze. Beneath it large, brightly coloured velvet cushions were strewn across a huge Persian rug. And in the middle, laid out on a low wooden table, was lunch.

Her hand flew up to her mouth.

Turning, Massimo studied her face as though assessing her reaction. 'I know I said I'd take you out to lunch, and I hope you're not disappointed, but I thought it would be more fun to have a picnic.'

His mood seemed to have lightened, and she felt a warm rush of relief. She didn't exactly know why, but she wanted him to feel happy. Maybe because he had made her happy. Her gaze drifted over the suckling pig, roasting over a pit of ash, and then moved back to the bottles of champagne chilling in a huge copper ice bucket. Who wouldn't be happy with this?

'It's not a picnic. It's a banquet!' she murmured.

'Are you sure you don't mind about the restaurant?' His face softened. Reaching out, he ran his thumb gently down her arm. 'I wanted it to be just the two of us. I didn't want to share you.'

His gaze slid slowly over her throat, dropping down to the curve of her breast, and then his eyes locked on to hers and she felt her heart beat faster beneath their shimmering, teasing gaze.

She breathed out slowly. He was probably just talking about sex again, but still, they could have just stayed on the yacht. So it had to have been his choice to bring her to this beautiful, idyllic beach...

Her shoulders stiffened. But perhaps he brought all his conquests here. After all, what woman could resist paradise?

'No,' he said softly, lifting up his hand to touch her face. 'I've never brought anybody else here. That's what you were thinking, wasn't it?'

She stared at him. 'There are a lot of islands in the world,' she said grittily.

'And there are a lot of women. But I haven't taken any of them to any island.' His eyes gleaming, he drew her into his arms. 'But I love it that you care that I might have done.'

'I *don't* care,' she lied, pushing him away. 'It would just be awkward if you'd left any of them behind.'

He burst out laughing and reached out for her. 'There are no women hiding in the bushes. I promise. But there's going to be one unhinged man on this beach if I don't eat soon!'

The food was delicious. After the crew had cleared away the plates and glasses with swift, soundless efficiency, Flora lay back on one of the cushions, her head resting on Massimo's shoulder. She was trying not to stare at him but it was difficult. With his shirt unbuttoned and his hair mussed up by the breeze drifting gently over the sand he looked more desirable than ever.

Feeling her gaze on his face, he leaned over and kissed her softly on the mouth. His lips were cold and tasted of honey and berries.

'Penny for them?' he said, tracing a finger up the bare skin of her thigh so that she squirmed against him.

'You'd get change,' she said lightly.

He frowned. 'What does that mean?'

She tilted her head back. He was watching her intently

and the feel of his eyes on her was making it difficult for her to breathe. 'It was something my mum used to say...' she said finally.

He waited for her to continue.

She shrugged. 'I don't know. I've been thinking about her a lot today. Before she died we used to go sailing together. Not your kind of sailing.' She gave him a quick, tight smile. 'We had a little dinghy and it was just the two of us. My dad and Freddie—my brother—they both got seasick, so it was just the two of us. Me and Mum.'

Glancing up at him, she hesitated, expecting him to look bored, but instead he nodded. 'When did she die?'

'When I was twelve. But she was ill for a couple of years before that.' Her shoulders tensed and she looked down at her hands.

'I'm sorry.'

He meant it. She could hear it in his voice.

She nodded. 'Me too.'

'So, do you still sail?'

His voice was so gentle that she had to curl her fingers into the palm of her hand to stop tears from filling her eyes. 'No. At first I didn't want to. But later my dad...' She paused. 'It made him worry. He couldn't help it,' she added almost defensively. 'He'd just lost my mum, and sailing *is* dangerous.'

'Did he remarry?'

Looking up, she was shaken by the intense blueness of his gaze. 'No. No, he didn't. He never really got over her death. You see, they were like soul mates.'

Trying to ignore the scratchiness in her voice, she gave him another quick, tight smile.

'They met at school. He was the year above her but *she* asked him out.' She bit her lip. 'He was just so lost without her. Some people can't be apart,' she said slowly.

She fell silent. Beside her, Massimo was silent too, and for a moment there was no sound except the waves washing over the sand. Looking across the beach, she watched the foam rise and fall, feeling awkward. Not that she really blamed him for having nothing to say. In her experience death was a no-go area for most people, and certainly not the most fitting topic of conversation for a picnic on a deserted island.

'My mother didn't really like the water very much.' His voice jolted her from her thoughts, and slowly she lifted her head. He smiled tautly.

'When she took me swimming she used to pile all her hair up on top of her head and do this incredibly slow breaststroke so as not to splash herself.'

Flora nodded but her head was spinning so fast she hardly knew what she was doing. Up until today Massimo had been like a dot-to-dot puzzle: she'd just filled in the lines, creating a picture of a man who was unscrupulous and ruthless. Only now she saw a different man. A man who'd once been a boy, struggling as she had with grief and guilt and loneliness and loss.

Leaning forward, Massimo ran his finger lightly over the pattern on the carpet. 'She had this sapphire necklace my father gave her when I was born and she always refused to take it off in the water. It drove my father mad. But he'd always back down. I think he liked it that she loved it so much.'

Flora looked at him. 'She sounds like she knew her own mind!'

'She did. She was very strong-willed.' His eyes met hers and he smiled reluctantly. And then his smile faded. 'She was strong too. Right up until the end she'd get dressed and do her hair and put on her make-up…'

'And her necklace?' she said softly.

Massimo nodded. His finger stopped moving. He'd never talked to anyone about his mother's death. When she'd died he'd been too young. And then later he'd been too angry. He felt sadness settle around his heart. It had been so long since he'd even spoken her name. He hadn't meant to do it, but in his grief for what he'd lost he'd edited her out of his life.

Chewing her lip, Flora stared up at his profile. He looked remote, untouchable, hard-edged. But she knew now that was how he'd learnt to manage the pain. Knew too that he hadn't always been that way.

Anxious not to break this new mood of intimacy between them, she breathed out quietly. It was strangely calming, sitting beside him, watching the play of sunlight beneath the canopy. Usually thinking about her mum left her feeling resentful and wrung out. But here, with the warmth of his body drawing her closer, she felt okay. Maybe it was because he actually understood how she felt; his mother's death had obviously had a huge impact on him. And his father too.

'How about your dad?' she said quietly. 'How did he cope after your mum died?'

Flora had a beautiful voice. Soft and husky and soothing, like the sound of summer rain, but nothing could relieve the pain caused by her innocent question. And nothing would ever induce him to share that pain with anyone.

Massimo gave a humourless laugh. 'He managed.' His voice was cool with a definite edge to it.

It was time to change the subject. Glancing across the beach, she said lightly, 'I don't know about you, but I quite fancy a swim.' Gripping his hand, she stood up, pulling him to his feet. 'The only trouble is I don't have a bikini. You don't have one on the boat I could borrow, do you?'

'I don't think you'd fit mine,' he said sadly.

She nipped his hand with her fingers. 'I didn't mean *you*...' She hesitated 'I just thought maybe one of your guests might have left one behind.' Colour was spreading over her cheeks and collarbone but she met his gaze defiantly.

He gave her a long, considering smile. 'By "guests", I suppose you mean female guests? But, as I've never taken a woman on the boat before today, I'm afraid I can't help you. If it's any comfort, I don't have any trunks with me either.'

He paused, his eyes roaming lazily over her body, and the sand seemed to shift beneath her feet. She felt as if she'd been drinking. Adrenaline and anticipation were spiralling up inside her like the curl of lemon in a martini. And fear too. Fear that she was confusing sensation for emotion. If this was going to work she needed to stay in control of herself. She needed to make it just about sex. Just as they'd agreed.

'In that case,' she said softly, 'I suppose I'll just have to go naked.'

The air was thickening around them like a sea storm about to break. Even the waves seemed to have stopped beating against the shoreline.

Breathing unsteadily, she took a step backwards and in one swift move pulled her dress over her head. Proudly, like some island princess, she stood in front of him, the green satin of her bra and panties gleaming like damp leaves beneath the shade of the canopy.

A dark flush stained his cheeks; his narrowed eyes sent darts of bright blue light over her skin.

With shock, Flora realised that she *liked* him looking at her like that.

Her pulse slowed. More than liked... It made her feel alive: wild and strong and beautiful. And she wanted him to keep looking. Wanted him to want her.

But every time they had sex everything got a little messier inside her head. It scared her how badly she wanted him. But what scared her more was the fear that she might grow careless—might grow to want more. She didn't want to care. She didn't want to feel *any* emotion. Emotion was dangerous. Watching her dad suffer had shown her exactly how dangerous. What she needed was pleasure and passion. Pure and simple.

Reaching round with a hand that shook slightly, she unhooked her bra and let it slip through her fingers.

'Last one to the sea has to swim home.'

Their eyes met, then before he could reply, she turned and ran towards the surf.

He caught her moments later, his arm around her waist as the water foamed over her feet.

'You cheated,' she said breathlessly as he pulled her against him, the damp fabric of his trousers slipping against her skin. 'You've still got your clothes on.'

They were deeper now, the water splashing against their knees. His eyes were shimmering with passion. 'That's your fault,' he said hoarsely. 'You make me break the rules.'

And then he pulled her closer and kissed her feverishly.

Her lips parted as his hands slid over her body, every touch sending an exquisite flickering flare of heat over her skin. Cupping his hands beneath her bottom, he lowered her into the water and then, raising her up again, put his mouth to her breasts and delicately licked the salty droplets from each swollen tip.

She gasped, her body jerking forward. Reaching for him blindly, she pressed his head against her nipple. But it wasn't enough. Heat was swelling inside her, impossible to ignore. Desperately, she grabbed his hand and pulled it between her shaking thighs.

This was what she needed. To clear her mind of conflict and doubt and fear. Maddened, she clenched his hand, pressing down hard against the knuckles. Heat spiked inside her and, reaching down, she pushed his fingers beneath the wet satin, bit down on his shoulder and shuddered, muscles spasming, her pulse beating against the palm of his hand.

She heard him groan, and as he reached into his trousers for protection she clawed clumsily at his belt. Panting, he held her still against him, his hands circling her waist, and then as his mouth covered hers he surged inside her.

She clung to him, her hands gripping the muscles of his arms, gasping into the sea breeze, and then she felt his lips brush the side of her face.

'Oh!' She gave a start of surprise as some tiny orange and white fish flickered swiftly through the water beside them.

'Rainbow wrasse,' Massimo said quietly. 'The tide must be going out. We ought to get back to the yacht.'

She nodded and let go of his arm. Their eyes met and for a moment he hesitated, and then, frowning, he pulled her against him, kissing her fiercely. As they broke apart he began to laugh softly.

Looking up at him, she frowned. 'Why are you laughing?'

He shook his head. 'This suit is dry clean only.'

She started to laugh too. 'Serves you right for not taking it off.'

He dropped a kiss lightly onto her forehead. 'You want to know what's even funnier...?'

'I didn't know you could actually launder money.' Picking up the damp five-hundred-euro note, Flora gazed at it thoughtfully. 'It's bad enough having to wash everything else. How's your wallet?'

Massimo rolled his eyes. 'Clean!' he said drily. 'As are my clothes.'

Flora giggled. They had returned to the yacht, showered, and made love again before making their way up to the lounge area on the foredeck. 'At least you left your phone behind. Otherwise that would have been ruined too.'

He nodded, but with a shiver she saw that his face had taken on the same blank, shuttered look as earlier. Reminding him about his phone had been a stupid thing to do, she thought miserably. No doubt it had also reminded him of all the hours he'd wasted with her today.

'I don't want to talk about my phone,' he said firmly. 'It reminds me of work. Look… We've only got a few hours of daylight left, so I thought maybe we could go and take a look at Caprera.'

He lounged back in his chair, and she saw with relief that his face had softened and that he was smiling. 'It should be right up your street. Unspoilt, wild and rugged. A bit like me!'

Flora poked him gently with her foot. 'You might be wild and rugged, but you are definitely spoilt.'

She gave a yelp as he leaned forward swiftly and caught her ankle with his hand. Slowly and deliberately, he wrapped his fingers around the heel of her foot.

'What exactly do you mean?'

Her lashes fluttered. 'I mean that you own an eighty-metre yacht—'

'She's actually eighty-*three* metres. I just rounded it down to make things easier for you.'

She rolled her eyes. 'Fine. You own an eighty-three-metre yacht, a *palazzo*. Probably a house—' He held up his hand and she frowned. 'You have *five* houses?'

Laughing he shook his head. 'Apartments—not houses.

And I have nine. I just couldn't hold up enough fingers. I thought you might kick me if I let go of your foot!'

She giggled. 'I have two feet, actually. Or did you round them down as well?'

He grinned and slid his hand down over her foot, pressing his thumb into the soft pad of flesh at the base of her toes.

Shifting in her seat, she tipped back her head. 'That feels amazing...' she mumbled.

'This part of the foot is supposedly connected to your neck,' he said slowly.

'That's *so* weird. My neck is actually tingling.'

She moaned softly. His fingers were caressing the underside of her heel, curling round to the hollow beneath her anklebone, drawing small, light circles over her skin. Leaning back against the chair, she felt boneless, her body melting beneath the sure, firm touch of his fingers.

And then her spine tightened and she arched upwards, heart pounding. 'What's *that* connected to?' she asked shakily.

'Can't you tell?' he murmured.

Her breath caught in her throat and, lifting her head, she stared at him dizzily. His eyes met hers and she swallowed at the dark intensity of their focus.

'Massimo. You can't—' She breathed out unsteadily.

But he could.

Soon his fingers had found the spot that made her squirm. Her heart was beating slow and hard, her thighs trembling, her breath coming in gasps. She shifted in her seat, desperate to ease the aching tightness in her pelvis, but his hand tightened, securing her. She wriggled helplessly, her whole body straining against his grip, but he kept stroking her with same deliberate, light touch.

'Please!' she gasped.

His eyes locked onto hers, and he loosened his grip. But only momentarily.

'I'll scream,' she said hoarsely.

He smiled. 'I know.'

And then he lowered his head, and her fingers splayed out across the arms of the chair as she felt his tongue start to circle her anklebone with merciless, measured precision. Rolling back in her seat, she let go, crying out softly as her body split apart and a bright, wild sweetness spread over her skin.

For a moment every thought was blotted out. From somewhere far away, or maybe nearby, she felt him reach forward and pull her towards him. Her hands twitching against the hard muscles of his stomach, she lay against him until finally her breathing returned to normal.

She'd had no idea that was even possible. Or that she would respond like that. Her face grew warm and, feeling slightly embarrassed by her lack of sexual sophistication, she shifted position.

And gasped.

He was hard—not just hard. The thickness of his erection pressing against her felt shockingly large. Looking up at him, eyes wide, she opened her mouth to speak but he stopped her, pressing his finger gently against her lips.

'It's fine,' he said quietly, his eyes clear and steady. 'I can wait. If it's you, I can wait for ever.'

CHAPTER EIGHT

MASSIMO'S WORDS HAD been more poetic than truthful, Flora admitted later as she stared out to sea, watching the sun slowly sink below the horizon. Not that she was complaining. It had been just as much her idea as his to keep things simple between them.

No feelings. No future. Just sex.

Well, she had certainly got what she wanted.

Having made it to his suite of cabins, they had spent the rest of the afternoon in bed, where Massimo had touched and teased her to orgasm after orgasm until finally she had pleaded exhaustion.

She felt her face grow warm. It had been so fierce, so intense. And so good. A fluttering rush like the wings of a hummingbird ran over her skin and, stretching out on the bed, she stared down at herself appraisingly. Then, pressing her legs together, she smiled, relishing the ache between her thighs.

Being with Massimo was a revelation. She'd enjoyed sex before, but she'd never realised it was possible to feel so *aroused*. It was an education—the positions, his intuitive understanding of what she would like. But it was more than that. *She* felt different when she was with him.

Flora curled her knees up to her chest and hugged them tightly. Of *course* she felt different. Massimo lived in another world. Of limousines and chauffeurs. Of helicopters and homes on several different continents. He was friends with people who owned islands—actual islands. It wasn't that his wealth mattered to her: it didn't. But there was no point pretending that she was oblivious to it either.

She heard the door open and, turning, she sat up and started to laugh as Massimo came in wearing a pair of swim shorts covered in large luminous green dollar signs.

'Are those yours? I'm not surprised you left them on the boat.'

He grinned at her. 'Sadly, I didn't. I thought we might want to use the pool later, so I sent Tommaso to go and buy us some swimwear.' He frowned. 'It was dollar signs or giant bananas. Apparently the selection was a little limited.'

She giggled. 'Was it, though? Was it *really*?'

'I suppose you'd have chosen the bananas?'

Still laughing, she met his eyes. 'Only if they didn't have any covered in very tiny chillies.'

He was still grinning. 'It's a pity you weren't there to help him choose. A *real* pity...' he said slowly.

She stared at him and then gave a yelp. 'What did he get for me? Show me!'

Her mouth dropped open as Massimo reached into the pocket of his trunks and pulled out what appeared to be nothing more than three tiny triangles of bright orange fabric.

She stared at it in horror. 'What is *that*?'

'It's a micro-bikini,' he said helpfully. 'Tommaso's girl-friend has one just like it. Only hers is pink.' His eyes gleamed. 'Bet you wish you had some trunks like mine now!'

She stuck her tongue out at him and, laughing, he dropped lightly onto the bed beside her and pulled her willing body against him.

Her pulse flickered. Even in those ridiculous shorts he looked utterly gorgeous, and his lean, tanned torso pressed snugly against her skin felt just as good as it looked.

Looking up, her heart gave a jolt as she met his gaze. His eyes were so blue that looking into them made her feel as though she were slipping beneath the sea. Instantly, her skin began to tingle.

'We could share,' she said huskily; her fingers were itching to touch him so badly she could hardly speak. 'Maybe.' He rubbed his face against hers, the bristles from his beard grazing her cheeks. 'It depends. What will you give me in return?'

Staring down at her, he felt a happiness he'd forgotten existed—sweet and cold and sharp like a shot of *limoncello*. She was so incredibly sexy. He loved how responsive she was to his touch. Sex with her was like no sex he'd ever had. His heartbeat slowed. But it wasn't just the sex. He *liked* her. She intrigued him; she made him laugh, and she teased him constantly, and yet this afternoon she'd managed to draw some of the pain from his heart.

Her hand slid over his stomach, her fingers tracing the line of dark hair disappearing beneath his shorts, and he pushed his thoughts away.

'What do you want?' she whispered.

In reply, he gave her a slow, sweet smile and began to tug deftly at the buttons of her shirt.

Somewhere across the room, his phone rang. His fingers faltered, and he glanced over his shoulder, feeling his stomach muscles knot together. It was his own fault. He should never have switched his phone back on. But either way he wasn't going to answer it.

He shrugged. 'It's fine. They can wait. If it's important they'll ring back.'

Flora nodded. He was probably right. But something in his voice made the hairs on the back of her neck stand up.

The phone was still ringing and, unable to stop herself, she said quickly, 'Why don't you answer it? I don't mind—'

'But I do,' he said flatly.

He could feel it starting to rise up inside him. That same dark misery he'd felt as a child. Except he wasn't a child any more, and he didn't have to explain himself to anyone.

Frowning, he shook his head. 'I didn't mean to snap. It's just—' The phone stopped and he breathed out sharply. 'It won't be important.'

She wanted to ask him how he knew, but deliberately he reached out, curving his hand under her chin. Lowering his face, he kissed her hungrily. *This* was what he wanted, he thought urgently. This was all he needed to make the rest of the world vanish. Just him and Flora. Untouchable. Perfect. Like a scene in a snow globe.

Except—except that he would never *need* anyone. Need was just another word for hurt. He'd needed his father and his father had betrayed him. He would never forgive nor forget that pain. But he knew a way to blot it out—

Flora gave a soft moan as he kissed her again, parting her lips roughly. She gave herself up to the shivering heat creeping over her skin and then her breath jolted in her throat as he jerked her closer. Some part of her brain registered that there was tension, almost anger in his gesture, but she pushed the thought away for his lips were soft and sure on hers, his fingers surer still as they slid under her shirt, seeking the hard peaks of her nipples—

The phone rang again and she felt him flinch. At the same moment he broke away from her, cursing angrily under his breath.

She stared at him unsteadily. His skin was stretched taut

across his cheekbones, his anger radiating to every corner of the room. She knew his fury and frustration weren't directed at her, but somehow that didn't make her feel much better. Biting her lip, she took a deep breath and touched him lightly on the arm. 'What is it?'

He didn't look at her, just shook his head. 'Nothing!'

The phone kept ringing and, running his fingers distractedly through his hair, he shook off her hand and stood up abruptly. It was intolerable. It was harassment.

'I'm not doing this—'

Flora gaped at him. Doing what? Was he talking to her? Or about the phone call?

She watched in silence as he strode across the room and snatched up the phone. Yanking open the door, he disappeared into the corridor and a moment later she heard his voice.

Crouching on the bed, she felt her stomach turn over with misery.

She'd seen him angry. When he'd been upset with her he'd been wild and stormy. But this was far worse. This anger was coldly controlled. His clipped, staccato voice as lethal and hostile as machine gun fire. What could have happened to make him that furious?

But the answer to that was obvious, she thought, and her own anger was cold and hard, like a small, sharp stone. For even without being able to hear what was being said, it didn't take a genius to work out that he was talking to a woman. Probably that Allegra girl he'd been so disparaging about in the café yesterday.

Her heart felt slow and heavy inside her chest. Was it only yesterday she'd sat in that café and listened to his lies? She felt a flicker of irritation. How could she have been so stupid? So gullible? All that talk of not wanting to share her when all the time he was fully intending to keep on sharing himself! But just because she might have been stupid enough to believe his lies once, it didn't mean she had to let him treat her like a fool now.

She let out a shaky breath. She felt cold and shivery, and if she'd been the crying type it would have been a good time to cry, but instead she stood up and padded across the room. Picking up her clothes, she dragged them over her limbs, barely registering whether they were inside out or upside down. She had just slipped her feet into her shoes when the door opened and Massimo walked in.

He stared at her blankly, almost as though he didn't recognise her. 'What are you doing?'

'Leaving,' she said coldly.

His eyes narrowed. 'Because I took a phone call?' He stared at her incredulously. 'Isn't that a little extreme?'

She took a quick breath. He was so manipulative! Twisting the facts and implying that she was overreacting when he'd just got off the phone from his girlfriend!

She glowered at him, so hurt and angry that she could hardly speak. 'I'll tell you what's extreme. Your selfishness. Just because you're rich and powerful and I'm not, it doesn't mean you can just use me—'

Massimo interrupted her sharply. 'How have I used you? We have an agreement—'

'*Had!*' she snapped back at him. 'I told you I was happy to have sex with you if there was no one else involved.'

The confusion on his face was so genuine, so convincing, that she wanted badly to believe him and some of her anger faded. She frowned. 'I heard you. You were arguing with someone—' Her anger flared again. 'And don't try and tell me it was work. I'm not an idiot.'

There was a long, strained silence, and then Massimo said quietly, 'No, you're not. But it's not what you think it is.'

Biting her lip, she looked away, her eyes drawn to a beautiful flame-coloured sunset outside the window. He was telling the truth. But it wasn't enough. She wanted—no, needed some kind of explanation.

'So who was it, then?'

His expression shifted. He met her gaze but didn't say anything. Finally, he shrugged. 'It doesn't matter.'

Her heart began to pound. 'How can you say that? Of *course* it matters. You were upset—'

'It's not your problem.'

Feeling numb inside, Flora forced herself to focus on the sunset. It was so beautiful, so simple. Just as today had been. Until now.

At what point had she become so stupid? She'd thought she was being so smart, so 'modern'. But seriously, how could she ever have thought this would work? Of course it had been easy in theory, agreeing just to have sex. But the reality was far more complicated and growing ever more so because the truth was she no longer just wanted him, she cared about him too.

Glancing at Massimo's still, set face, she swallowed what felt like a hard little lump in her throat. She cared that he was hurting. Even now, when he'd made it perfectly clear that he didn't want or need her help, she still cared.

Because she liked him.

She liked him a lot, she thought miserably.

She might only have intended to share her body with him, but now she was in danger of sharing her heart. The lump in her throat swelled. Except that he didn't want her heart. And, judging by the closed expression on his face, he certainly didn't want to share his feelings.

Watching her swallow, Massimo gritted his teeth. He knew he was hurting her. But he didn't know what else to do. He couldn't tell her truth. Let her stay as she was:

soft and light, shimmering with promise like the dawn of a spring morning. There was no need to blight her life by revealing how cruel the world really was.

But even though he couldn't tell her the truth about the past, he could tell her how he was feeling now.

'I didn't mean to upset you, *cara*. Truly, it's the last thing I want to do...' He hesitated and stepped towards her. 'If I could tell you I would. But I can't. Please don't hate me for that.'

She looked up at him, her gaze searching his face, and he felt his heart contract with shock—for there was no hatred in her eyes, just something that unbelievably looked like concern.

'I don't hate you,' she said quietly. 'I just don't understand you. And that seems like a reason to leave to me.'

His heartbeat slowed. She was wavering. He could hear it in her voice. Impulsively, he leaned forward and pulled her closer. She pushed her hands against his chest, but it was a token gesture of resistance. Feeling a rush of triumph, he closed the gap between them.

'I don't understand me either,' he said softly. 'But I do know that I don't want to fight with you.' He shook his head. 'I want it to be like it was earlier.'

She bit her lip and then nodded slowly. 'I do too.'

He watched a flush of colour spread over her cheeks and, feeling a sudden overwhelming need to touch her, he reached out and gently stroked her face.

She looked so young and, remembering the sadness in her eyes when she'd told him about her mother's death, he felt a sudden urge to protect her. To turn the yacht out to sea and sail away into that glorious, cinematic sunset.

He sighed. 'I'm sorry. I know I said we could spend the night on the boat but we can't,' he said slowly. 'I forgot I've got a dinner. Tonight. And I can't not be there. It's business. Well, politics and business. I'm having dinner with the prime minister.'

Watching her eyes widen in shock, he shook his head. He still couldn't quite believe that it had slipped his mind. It had certainly never happened before. Eyeing him sideways, Flora felt a rush of disappointment but as he met her gaze, she held out her hand.

'It's fine. Give me that bikini. I can swim home.'

She was back to teasing him. Relief swept over him and then swiftly faded. He didn't want to leave her behind. Nor did he want to be stuck in some soulless hotel room with just the mini-bar and his thoughts for company.

But why should he be alone?

He slid his arm around her waist and pulled her firmly against him. 'How would you like to go to Rome with me?'

'I think—perhaps—if we do this...' Frowning, Massimo got to his feet and, standing in front of Flora, folded the shimmering blue fabric below her collarbone. 'Would that work?'

Elisabetta, the tiny and incredibly chic head assistant at the Via dei Condotti fashion house, nodded approvingly. 'It would indeed, Signor Sforza.' With swift fingers, she deftly pinned the silk in place and then, turning to Flora, she smiled. 'Perhaps you would like to see yourself now, *signorina*?'

Smiling weakly back at her, Flora nodded and stepped tentatively in front of the mirror. She stared at herself in silence, jolted by her reflection.

It fitted perfectly. As it should, she thought wryly, after two hours of pinning and pinching. It was all so exciting. She'd never had a dress made for her before, and she'd loved every moment. More exciting though was the way Massimo had dominated the huge fitting room, not a single stitch escaping his glittering blue gaze.

Watching him, it had been easy for her to see why he was so successful in business: he had given her dress the same focus as he gave to driving his sports car or teasing her to orgasm with his tongue.

And lucky for her that he did, she thought, gazing raptly at her reflection in the trio of huge mirrors that lined one end of the room. The dress was utterly divine.

She caught sight of Massimo watching her in the mirror and blushed. 'Thank you,' she said softly. 'It's lovely, really, and incredibly generous of you.'

He took a step closer, his eyes never leaving her face. 'It's my pleasure. Truly. And the dress *is* lovely, but it would be nothing without you, *cara*. You take my breath away.'

She smiled mechanically. His voice was soft, his gaze softer still, but that didn't make his remark true any more than it made the evening a date.

Heart hammering, desperate not to let him see how much she wanted his words to be true, she reached up and pressed a trembling finger against his lips. 'Then don't say any more,' she said lightly. 'I don't want you collapsing on me.'

It had been like a rollercoaster ride.

They had flown to Rome in Massimo's helicopter and a chauffeur-driven limousine had met them at the airport and whisked them across the city to the salon just as it had been about to close. It was yet another reminder that Massimo was no ordinary man. And that in his world shops were always open, restaurants always serving food.

Now the limousine was slipping smoothly through the traffic-clogged streets. She blinked as a flash of blue light swept past them.

'I still can't believe we've got a police escort. I thought only world leaders had those.'

Massimo squeezed her hand. 'I don't normally have one. But we're guests of the prime minister; that's why security's a little over the top.'

Lounging beside her like a modern-day Roman emperor in a dinner jacket and dress shirt, he looked as though he could rule not just the country but the universe, she thought helplessly. He was just so perfect. As though sensing her focus, he turned, his gaze locking onto her and horrified that he might actually be able to read her thoughts, she took refuge in humour. 'It certainly is. Your ego is bulletproof. You certainly don't need any encouragement—'

She broke off, her breath snagging in her throat, as he jerked her towards him and she felt the hard length of his arousal through his trousers.

'Not with you, I don't.' He groaned softly. 'I can't bear being this close to you and not being able to do anything.'

She felt her skin began to burn as his eyes roamed slowly and appreciatively over the clinging silk, and then she shivered as he slid his hand through the slit in the back of her dress and pressed his cool palm against her hot bare flesh.

'And I am definitely not going to be able to keep my hands off you in that dress for much longer—'

There was a discreet cough over the intercom.

Gritting his teeth, Massimo looked up sharply towards the front of the car.

'We're nearly there, sir,' said the chauffeur. 'There are quite a lot of photographers, so do you want me to take you to the front or use the service entrance—?'

'The front entrance will be fine.'

'What *is* this place?' Flora said shakily. She had never seen so many paparazzi or security guards.

'The Palazzo del Quirinale. It's the official residence of the Italian President,' Massimo said smoothly.

'I thought we were meeting the Prime Minister?'

'We are. And the President too.'

She bit her lip. 'Is that all?'

He hesitated. 'No. Not exactly.'

She stared at him nervously. 'How many other people are going?'

'Not many. Probably about fifty or sixty,' he said casually. Her mouth fell open, but it was too late to say anything now. They had arrived. The car slid smoothly to a stop and he gave her hand a quick squeeze.

'I'll be with you the whole time,' he said firmly.

As the doors opened she smoothed her dress down over her legs and stepped out onto the road into a roar of sound. Around her camera flashes exploded in every direction, and then Massimo was by her side, his hand locked tightly in hers.

'Don't look so worried. Just keep looking at me like you're crazy about me!'

His eyes gleamed, and she pinched him on the arm. 'I'm a gardener. Not an actress!'

'You won't need to act.'

He grinned at her, that sweet, slow grin that made her skin slip from her bones, and then, lowering his head, he kissed her. Lights flashed. But whether or not they were just inside her head she couldn't tell. All she knew was that there was nothing and no one that mattered but him and the fierce pressure of his kiss.

He lifted his head. 'See! No acting required,' he murmured.

His eyes were the darkest blue, as though he'd swallowed the night sky. She stared at him in confusion, her body tingling, her head still swimming. Behind them the photographers were calling out Massimo's name, and with shock she realised that it wasn't just the two of them any more. This wasn't the kitchen at the *palazzo* or even his yacht. This was public. It was *real*.

She felt a sharp stab of longing. Did that mean it was more than sex for him too now?

'Wh-why did you do that?' she said shakily.

Taking her hand, he led her along the red carpet, past the lines of security guards.

'We're in the city of love, *cara*. What else could I do?'

She gazed up at him, transfixed by the light in his eyes. 'I thought Paris was the city of love?'

He frowned and shook his head slowly. 'A Frenchman told you that, right?' He sighed. 'I'd be charitable and say he made a mistake, but I know that guy and he is not to be trusted. Rome is *definitely* the city of love.'

It was only later that she realised he'd been trying to distract her, no doubt prompted by her poorly concealed panic. But despite her nerves she started to relax—in the main because at every opportunity Massimo materialised by her side and slid his hand into hers. Almost as though he wanted everyone to know she was with him. Although that was most likely wish fulfilment on her part rather than fact.

'Thank goodness,' he muttered in her ear as the doors to the dining room opened. 'Don't worry—I tipped one of the waiters to put us next to one another. That way I can make sure you don't run off with the Minister for Trade!'

The Minister for Trade turned out to be a large, florid man in his mid-sixties, whose wife was sitting next to Massimo.

'She seemed nice,' Flora said later as they sat in the *salon della feste* enjoying their coffees.

'Carla? Yes, she is. They both are. It's his second marriage. His first wife died. They had a daughter about your age who's in a bit of a mess. She's not really coping.'

Flora bit her lip. 'That's so sad.'

He nodded, his eyes resting on her face. 'I hope you don't mind, but I told her about you.'

'You did?'

'I thought maybe you could talk to her. You don't mind, do you?'

She shook her head. 'No. I don't mind. But I'm not sure how much use I'd be.'

He frowned. 'What do you mean?'

Stalling, she picked up her coffee. 'I'd feel like a fraud,' she said stiffly. 'It's not as if I'm *really* coping.'

There was a brief silence, and then Massimo leaned forward. 'Why do you think that?' he asked quietly.

She shrugged. The air was shifting around them—thickening, tightening. 'Because if I was I'd be at home in England.' She put down her coffee cup. 'I only came out here in the first place because I couldn't cope with being at home.' She sighed. 'My dad and my brother were always quite protective when I was growing up. But after my mum died they just completely stopped listening to me.'

Looking up, she gave him a small, stiff smile.

'They treat me like a five-year-old. So in the end I ran away. I told them it was so I could get my head together and finish my thesis. But really it was to get away from them.'

A faint flush of pink crept over her cheeks.

'That's why I got on so well with Umberto. I know what everyone thought. But we were never lovers. We just understood each other: he was on the run too. From his wives and his mistresses. And the fact that he couldn't paint like he used to. So you see I didn't cope. I ran away.'

She fell silent. Around them the noise of laughter and people talking swelled and faded like a tide.

'Could you talk to your dad, maybe? Or Freddie?'

His voice was gentle. *Too* gentle. She felt her chest grow tight. How could she explain her father's grief? If *she* was struggling then he was hanging on by a thread. And Freddie was a lawyer. If she spoke to him she'd just end up agreeing with him as she always did.

'It would hurt him,' she whispered. 'And he's so broken. So fragile.'

Just thinking about her father, his face still anxiously scanning crowds, hoping for a glimpse of her mother, made her want to cry.

'I don't ever want to be that reliant on anyone,' she said angrily. 'What's the point of loving someone and caring for them if it makes you feel like that?'

She looked up at him, but he'd glanced away to where the waiters were clearing tables, and she felt despair, sudden and sharp enough to cut her skin. Of course! Why would Massimo be interested in her pain?

'It's what makes life worth living.'

His voice was so quiet at first she thought she might be hearing things.

But then he turned and said softly, 'If you don't feel sad when someone isn't there… If you don't care if they're happy or not…then there's no point.'

His eyes fixed on hers and, leaning across, he took her hand and pressed it against his mouth.

'Mr Sforza—?'

Flora turned and looked up dazedly. It was one of the waiters.

Massimo stared at him coolly. 'What is it?'

'I have a telephone call for you, sir.'

It was as though a switch had been flicked. Flora froze as Massimo shifted in his seat, his jaw tightening.

'Can't you see we're busy?'

His tone was so harsh she was surprised it didn't strip the gilt off the salon's golden walls. Glancing at Flora's frozen expression, the waiter hesitated.

'I'm sorry, sir. But there's been an accident—'

Massimo's face went white. 'Is she hurt?'

The waiter shook his head. 'I don't know, sir—'

Massimo turned to Flora. 'Wait here. I'll be back as soon as possible.'

She'd barely had a chance to drain her cup of coffee when he reappeared looking, if possible, angrier than he had on the yacht.

She got to her feet. 'Is she okay?' She had no idea who this mysterious 'she' was but she could feel Massimo's pain and she wanted to help him.

He stared at her, his features distorted with pure, blank-eyed rage. 'Of *course* she's okay. She lied just to get me to come to the phone.

Flora felt her heart start to pound. What kind of person would lie about being in an accident?

'Why would she—?'

'I don't want to talk about it,' he said coldly, his voice as flat and dangerous as black ice. She stared at him numbly, seeing the anger in his eyes and for a moment she hesitated. They'd already had a huge row that day. And some problems were just too big to solve. Like her father's grief...

Her stomach tightened. She hadn't wanted to deal with her dad's misery or his over-protectiveness so instead of confronting him, she'd run away. Feeling something like shame or guilt prod her in the ribs, she lifted her chin. This time though, she wasn't going to run away.

'Tough!' she said slowly. 'You can't just expect me to ignore this, Massimo. What's the big secret? Why won't you tell me who keeps ringing you?'

'I'm not prepared to discuss it with you,' he said roughly.

'But you *are* prepared to have sex with me?' she snapped.

Around them the room fell quiet. There was a moment of tense, expectant silence and then everyone began speaking at once.

They stared at each other for a moment, and then his eyes slipped away across the salon.

'Fine,' he said, his breath catching savagely on the word. 'Have it your way! But not here.'

He grabbed her roughly by the hand and dragged her out of the salon. He was walking so fast she had to run to keep up with his strides. Glancing up at his set, cold face, she felt dread scuttle across her skin.

What had she done?

But it was too late for regrets. Pushing open a door, he pulled her through with him, and suddenly they were outside.

He stopped and dropped her hand as though it were burning him. Glancing round, she saw that they were on a huge, terraced balcony and beyond that there was nothing but darkness.

She could hear his breathing—sharp, unsteady—and, turning slowly, she stared at his profile.

'Who is she?'

There was a silence, and then finally he said curtly, 'She's my stepmother.' He turned and looked at her. 'Her name's Alida.'

The rawness in his voice made her wince, but she said as calmly as she could, 'Why won't you speak to her?'

He laughed—a harsh laugh without any humour in it whatsoever. 'Because she made my life a misery.'

She hesitated. 'When did she marry your dad?'

His lip curled back into a snarl. 'Just after my mother died. When I was five.'

Watching his body tense, she shivered. She knew he

was remembering the hurt and the loneliness in every nerve and muscle, and the misery on his face made her feel sick.

'Is that why you were sent to boarding school?'

His eyes, narrowed and hostile like a cornered animal's, met hers. 'She told my father she couldn't manage me. That I was too difficult to handle.'

Flora felt a knot in her stomach. 'But you were only five,' she said slowly, 'and your mum had just died. I don't understand. Why didn't your dad stand up to her...?'

Her voice trailed off as Massimo's mouth curved into a grim smile.

'My father always took the path of least resistance. I don't think he wanted to oppose her. He hated rows, confrontation—'

'But surely he didn't want you to go away?'

A muscle jumped in his cheek and he stared out into the darkness. 'I don't know what he wanted. After he married Alida I barely saw him.' His eyes glittered coldly. 'I spent most holidays at school. When I was allowed home they went away travelling. I used to get sent to live with my father's handyman and his wife.'

Her head was spinning. But she needed to stay focused. Her shock and horror were not important beside his pain.

'What happened next?'

His mouth twisted. 'He died when I was sixteen. The last time I saw him properly was about five months before his death. I was summoned so he could tell me he'd changed his will.' The anger had faded from his voice. There was nothing in it now—no life, no feelings and tears rose in her throat.

'You can probably guess in whose favour.'

He made a movement somewhere between a shrug and

a shiver and fell silent, leaning back against the wall as though exhausted.

Flora breathed out shakily. It was cruel. More than cruel, it was abusive. How could anyone treat a child like that? It was incomprehensible. Alida was obviously selfish and spiteful, but Massimo's father— She shivered. How did anyone survive a betrayal like that? But with shock, she realised she knew how: by offering love and support.

Except that there didn't seem to be much of that in Massimo's life.

He had money and power, the envy and respect of his rivals and the admiration of his staff. But nothing approximating to tenderness or care. Even his many affairs seemed to have offered him nothing more than sexual gratification.

He was like a plant that had been forced to survive in the darkest, driest corner of a garden. If only he *was* a plant, she thought helplessly. It would be so much easier. She would know exactly what to do.

Even before her brain had started to process that thought her body responded and, leaning forward, she slid her arms around him. For a moment he didn't move, and then slowly he pressed her against him.

And there, wrapped in his arms, she knew.

Knew without a shred of doubt or denial that she loved him. Her heart missed a beat. Surely it couldn't be true.

Love was dangerous. Love hurt. Even years after her mum's death, her father was still tormented by her loss. But she saw now that none of that mattered. All her fears and all those careful plans she'd made to stay single and safe had been for nothing. She didn't get to choose. Her heart did. And, no matter how disastrous the consequences might be for her, it had chosen Massimo.

Words of joy bubbled up inside her but she stemmed the

flow. There had been enough talking for one night. Right now Massimo needing some tender loving care, and what she had in mind didn't require words.

She felt his lips brush across her hair and, looking up, she smiled. 'Let's go home.'

CHAPTER NINE

It was the early hours of the morning when they walked back into the *palazzo*.

Tired though she was, Flora didn't think she'd ever been happier. Yes, they'd quarrelled, and it had been difficult and upsetting, but for the first time sex hadn't been their 'go-to' to blot out the pain of the past or resolve the tension between them. Instead, they had talked and faced Massimo's demons together.

No longer two people just having sex. But equals coming together, side by side, to take on the world.

Walking up the stairs to his bedroom, Massimo kissed her with a tenderness and soft warmth that seemed to Flora to complement perfectly the golden glow of the dawn and their new mood of openness.

His eyes steady on hers, he touched her face almost reverently, his thumb brushing lightly over the smooth skin of her cheeks. And then, coaxing her lips apart with his tongue, his breath quick and warm against her mouth, he kissed her. It was a kiss she would remember all her life. A kiss that tasted of hope and dappled sunlight and everything crisp and green and new.

The sex felt different too, the incredible, raw physical attraction they felt for one another deepening into something more intimate, something bred from trust and openness. Riding a wave of sensation and arousal, they made love slowly, letting the memories of the past slip away in each other's arms, leaving only pleasure and longing behind. It felt like the most glorious dream... Time ceased to matter...sharp edges blurred into spinning circles of colour and light...

She didn't remember falling asleep.

But waking beside him, his body curved around hers, she knew that it hadn't been a dream. It was real. He'd even suggested that she return to Rome with him for a couple of days so he could show her the sights properly.

Wriggling down into the warmth of the bed, she felt a rush of happiness. Beside her, he shifted in his sleep and, looking over at him, she felt her breath catch in her throat. Sleeping, he looked younger, more defenceless—and she shivered, remembering everything he'd told her last night.

Even now the facts of his childhood horrified her, for she knew now how much it had damaged the adult Massimo. She knew too how much it must have cost him to reveal the truth to her. To trust her with his pain. A tiny hope sparked inside her. But he had trusted her *and* needed her. Needed her for more than just sexual gratification.

That had to mean something, didn't it?

She breathed out softly. Last night he had let her in; he'd shown her the 'real' Massimo. Not the über-cool, autocratic billionaire businessman, polished and harder than a diamond, but the man beneath the image.

The man she loved.

Her heart contracted and suddenly she wanted to leap out of bed and cartwheel around the room.

Was this how love felt?

Was this really what she'd been hiding from all these years?

She stared up at the ceiling, feeling reckless and wild

and alive. If she'd been an artist, like Umberto, she would have tried to paint her emotions. Just to see what they looked like. But instead she lay on her side and watched the sunlight and shadows play slowly across Massimo's face.

She loved him.

Frowning, she closed her eyes, shaken by how obvious it was to her now that what she'd been feeling for him was love.

It hardly seemed possible.

For so long she had pushed away all thoughts of ever giving her heart to anyone. She'd had boyfriends, but nothing that serious or permanent. In fact, in the past few years, she'd probably been closest to Umberto, and she hadn't even been romantically involved with him. Not that she had minded. She'd been content to watch others fall in love; she'd never wanted more.

Until now.

Until Massimo.

She breathed out slowly. When her mum had died it had been as if a fuse had blown inside her head. Alone and confused in the dark, she'd started to fear what lay outside. But Massimo had changed everything. He had brought light and hope into the darkness.

And she knew now that she'd rather feel *everything* with him—happiness *and* despair—than nothing on her own. He was worth the risk.

But would he feel the same way?

Feeling suddenly impossibly restless, she slid out of bed quietly, so as not to wake him, tugged on a pair of denim shorts and a T-shirt and tiptoed towards the door. It was too difficult to lie beside him, hoping that he might wake up feeling what she was feeling. Particularly when she'd barely come to terms with those feelings herself.

In the kitchen, she paced nervously around the table,

trying to order her thoughts. They barely knew one another, and up until a few hours ago their relationship had been based almost entirely on sex. It would be foolish, not to say disastrous, for her to imagine that was a good foundation for a future together.

But what was happening inside her head and her heart had nothing to do with sex. It was love.

Why else would she no longer want to fight with him—but *for* him? And why else would she finally be ready to pull down the emotional barriers she'd built to protect herself from the pain of caring?

In the past, she had been so scared of getting hurt, it had been easy to corral her emotions, to keep her distance. But being with Massimo had made her want to get closer. He'd quelled her fears, unlocked her life and given her the chance to dream again.

A sweet, shimmering happiness spread over her skin and suddenly she wanted him to know. Wanted him to know that she loved him and share her happiness.

Heart pounding, she turned towards the door—just as her stomach gave a loud rumble. Except she couldn't do it on an empty stomach. She would need a strong cup of coffee first. Or better still, some eggs and bacon!

Stifling a yawn, Massimo rolled onto his side. From downstairs he heard the sound of water running, cupboard doors shutting and, leaning over, he picked up his watch. He frowned. It was nearly two o'clock in the afternoon! Still, it was hardly surprising they'd slept in so late. They hadn't got to bed until three. He gave a smile of pure masculine satisfaction. Or to sleep until five.

His smile faded. It wasn't just their fevered lovemaking that had wiped him out. Last night had been emotionally draining too. He'd pretty much told her everything about his past: every hellish detail. He hadn't planned to—he still didn't really understand how he'd ended up doing so—but...

He braced himself against the bed. Until he'd met Flora his childhood had always been a locked room inside his head. And for good reason. His memories had power: the power to make him feel like a desperate, unhappy little boy again. Thinking about it, let alone discussing it with anyone, had simply not been an option. And he'd worked hard to keep it that way.

But somehow, yesterday, Flora had not only picked the lock, she'd kicked the damn door off its hinges.

How had she managed to do that? To blow his mind, his life, wide open like that?

Probably because she'd known grief too, he thought quickly. It had nothing to do with who she was as a person. Remembering her anxious face watching his, he shifted uncomfortably in the bed. Except that it did! She had put her own grief to one side and let him rage. She had listened, and she had forced him to face his feelings, and somehow that had lessened their power to hurt him. She hadn't actually held his hand, but she had been there by his side. And instead of feeling claustrophobic, it had felt liberating. His breathing slowed.

What if she was always there? By his side?

His phone juddered on the bedside table, and still reeling from the idea that his relationship with Flora could be more than just a no-strings fling, he picked it up without thinking. Glancing at the screen, he froze.

There were eleven messages.

All from Alida.

Deep inside he felt a familiar shifting sensation—a sense that his footing was not stable—he frowned. But why? Last night, Flora had helped him face the past: now he would face the present. And this time it would be different. He would be different: calm, detached, unassailable.

Standing up, he took a deep breath and punched a number into his phone.

'Finally! I would have thought you could have at least rung to see how I was.'

Even though he'd known what to expect, her voice sliced through his nerves like a scalpel. It was as polished and deadly as her glossily painted fingernails, and instantly he felt his bravado fail and once again, he was small and young and stupid.

Breathing out jerkily, his fingers tightened around the phone. 'I thought we agreed last night it wasn't serious?'

He heard her laugh—a tight, bitter sound that made his heart bang against his ribs.

'You mean compared to dining with the Prime Minister?'

He swallowed. 'There wasn't anything I could do—'

'There never is. Not now. Now you're far too important to be bothering with me.' Her voice was spiralling higher and higher. 'Too busy making all that money and sleeping with all those women to have time to talk to *me*.'

'I spoke to you yesterday—'

'You lost your temper with me yesterday! I can't imagine what your father would have said if he was still alive.'

'Can't you? I think that's highly unlikely. He'd have said exactly what you told him to say.'

Even before he'd finished speaking he knew his tone had come out more accusatory and emotional than he'd intended.

'Oh, here we go.'

He flinched. She was spitting the words down the phone at him, bile and bitterness ricocheting over the line.

'You needed boundaries. I was simply supporting your father. And you were so difficult to love. Always crying or having a tantrum. *Poor little Massimo!* Only you're *not* poor, are you? You're rolling in money. But what do I see of it? You barely send me enough to keep a cat alive—'

He was shivering uncontrollably, his heart beating like a trapped bird.

'I'll arrange for some money to be transferred this morning,' he heard himself say. 'I have to go now—'

With a hand that shook slightly he switched off his phone and sat down on the bed.

Earlier, he had felt so calm—lighter, almost. But the conversation with Alida had changed everything. Now his heart was racing, his nerves screaming like a car alarm.

How could he have been so stupid? Telling Flora about his past had been foolhardy and self-indulgent—for surely that same past had taught him that letting someone into your life, your head and, worse, your heart was tantamount to giving them control over you. He felt sick to his stomach. Look at how his father had changed after marrying Alida. Look at how Alida still knew exactly which buttons to press to make him feel helpless and trapped—

He should have followed his instincts to keep his private life private. Confiding in Flora had undermined all the efforts he'd made to keep control of his life. It had been careless, reckless even—he winced. How could he have thought he might want something other than sex with Flora?

He gritted his teeth. She'd caught him off guard. But it wouldn't happen again.

He couldn't let himself feel differently. Any more than he could alter his past. What he and Flora had was purely physical. He knew that now. And he needed to remind her of that fact as soon and as firmly as possible.

Picking up his clothes, he began to get dressed.

* * *

Humming softly, Flora picked up the heavy cast-iron skillet and put it on the hotplate. Next she filled the kettle with water and put it beside the skillet. Frowning, she looked round for the coffee pot. It wasn't in its normal place at the back of the stove. Nor was it in the dishwasher.

Bending over, she opened the doors of the huge dresser that nearly reached the ceiling and peered along the shelves. It wasn't there either. Sighing, she straightened up—and found Massimo watching her intently.

'Hi!'

She stared at him uncertainly. Despite privately acknowledging her feelings for him, she didn't really know what to expect from Massimo. Some awkwardness, maybe. But definitely closeness, given what they'd shared last night. Only he didn't seem awkward. Nor did he seem particularly inclined to be intimate. Standing just inside the doorway, hands deep in the pockets of his jeans, he looked more wary than anything.

His manner set her teeth on edge. It was hard to believe that she had been about to cook this man breakfast. Let alone tell him that she loved him.

But last night had been pretty intense for both of them. Probably he just needed a little time to relax.

'I can't find the coffee pot. The blue one,' she said, turning back towards the dresser. 'Have you seen it?'

He shook his head. 'No. But it might be in my study.'

He walked slowly across the room, his impassive face jarring against her nervous, hopeful excitement and quite suddenly the kitchen felt small and oppressive. 'I'll go and get it,' she said hurriedly. 'You can get the bacon—I mean the pancetta—out of the fridge.'

Standing in the hallway, she breathed out slowly. It had all felt so clear and right earlier.

Loving him had felt right.

Only now she wasn't so sure.

He was acting so strangely. Aloof and on edge—almost as though he was waiting to say something...

Pushing open the door to the room Massimo had appropriated for an office, she saw the coffee pot immediately. It was on his desk.

Sighing, she picked it up and turned to leave—and then, glancing down at the papers scattered across his desk, she felt the handle start to slip from her fingers. She gripped it more tightly. Inside her chest her heart had started to pound painfully hard.

She must be mistaken...but she knew she wasn't.

Massimo had moved. He was standing next to the stove, staring across the kitchen, his eyes dark and unreadable.

As she walked through the door he looked up at her, and she felt a surge of fury at his cool expression.

Trying to hold on to her temper, she put the coffee pot down on the worktop with exaggerated care and then casually, almost as an afterthought, dropped the plans she'd found in his study onto the kitchen table.

'These were on your desk.'

She felt it in the air first: the shift between them, the quivering rise in tension. Suddenly the room seemed to shrink around them.

Looking up, she met his gaze. 'They're plans for a development. Here. At the *palazzo*. But then you knew that, didn't you?' Her throat seemed to have closed up. Lifting her hand, she pressed it against her neck. 'I'm just wondering why didn't you tell me?'

Even saying the words hurt so much she could hardly breathe. He had held her in his arms, pushed inside her body, and yet he'd kept this from her.

How could he have *done* that?

Furiously, she realised how naive she'd been. At first, she'd assumed Massimo wanted the house for himself. Later, his furious determination to get her out was finally explained when the plans to convert the *palazzo* into a hotel were made public. But it had never occurred to her that there might be an even bigger picture.

But there was. And it was much, much bigger than she could have ever have imagined.

She looked back at the plans and shock hit her again like a punch to the stomach. Anger was rising inside her. And outrage too. These weren't plans for a development.

They were plans for an occupation.

'This is my home. You can't just decide that you want to knock it down and build some massive resort in its place.' Her voice was rising. 'There must be nearly fifty villas on those plans. And a golf course. It's huge—'

Massimo's eyes narrowed, his gaze on her flushed, angry face. Part of him knew that her anger was justified. And that she deserved some kind of explanation at the very least. But something cold twisted in his stomach. Why should he have told her anything? Or explain himself then or now? This was *his* property and she was nothing more than a tenant.

Just because last night she'd coaxed him into sharing grisly details about his childhood it didn't mean that he owed her anything. He shrugged.

'I don't know what you want me to say.'

Leaning back against the stove, he stared at her coldly. This was the only kind of conversation he liked. One that required cool detachment and logic. And absolutely no mercy.

Flora flinched and then her eyes flared. 'How about, "Flora, I thought you might be interested to know that I'm going to demolish your home and build a massive resort and golf course instead"?'

'Why would I tell you anything about the resort? It's none of your business,' he said coldly.

'How do you work *that* out?' She stared at him, feeling slightly sick. 'In the first place, I live here...'

Her voice faded as he shook his head slowly.

'Even without consulting a lawyer, I can tell you that your tenancy agreement is meaningless. It's certainly not going to stand in the way of hundreds of jobs, or the money this resort will bring to the community here.'

There was something soft and dangerous growing in his voice, but her own anger felt more acute, more pressing and so she ignored it.

'Is that all you think about? Jobs and money?' Her skin was trembling with rage, and the sort of hurt she hadn't felt since her mum died.

He shrugged. 'What else is there?'

She almost laughed. Only the pain and anger tangling inside her wasn't funny.

'There's *me*!'

He didn't move, but something flared in his eyes— something dark and formless. 'And who are *you* to tell me how to run my business?'

'I don't want anything to do with your damn business. But I thought...' She hesitated, her hands curling into fists at her sides. Did she really have to spell it out?

His gaze met hers and her stomach plummeted.

Apparently she did.

She lifted her chin. 'I thought I was something to do with your life. I can see why you wouldn't tell me at the beginning, but I thought things were different now. Between us. So why didn't you tell me after everything changed?'

'I didn't tell you because nothing has changed. Not with my plans for this building. Or with us,' he said coldly. His face was expressionless, but there could be no mistaking the distance in his eyes. 'It couldn't. Because there is no "us".'

For a moment her voice wouldn't work. Anger was clawing inside her like an animal, trying to climb out of a pit. 'How can you say that?' she said, her voice high and shaking. 'We haven't just been sleeping together. We've shared meals; we went to Rome—'

He looked at her incredulously. 'When I said we were just going to have sex, I didn't mean that literally. I'm not a Neanderthal.' Flora blinked. His eyes were staring through her, as though he had already deleted her from his life. 'But that doesn't make this a relationship.'

Shock and anger and misery rose in her throat, and for a second she thought she was going to throw up. 'But what about yesterday and last night?'

'What about it?'

Watching her eyes widen with shock and hurt, his skin tightened. He'd been right: he'd let her get too close. That was why she was so angry at him now. And that was why he needed to make sure she never did it again. Letting her know that his plan for the resort was off-limits was as good a way as any of proving to her that she was in his life for one reason and one reason only.

She stared at him wordlessly. She knew how hard it had been for him to tell her about his father and stepmother's treatment of him. So why was he acting now as though none of it had mattered?

A white ball of anger was swelling inside her chest and she swallowed, battening down the pain. 'Didn't what happened between us mean anything to you?'

His eyes on hers were cold, incurious. 'It was just a conversation—'

'It was *not* just a conversation.' She interrupted him,

eyes blazing. 'I told you things about myself, and you told me about your dad and your stepmother. We *shared* something.'

'Yes. Too much alcohol and too little sleep.'

The chill in his voice made her feel faint.

'Why are you being like this?' She breathed out unsteadily. 'Something happened between us. I know it did. I felt it, and I know you felt it too.'

Her heart was pounding but she wasn't going to walk away from this without a fight. Massimo found it difficult to trust. She knew that was why he was in denial about what had happened between them. All she needed was to find some way to make him trust her.

'I know what you're doing,' she said carefully. 'I know you want to push me away. And I know *why* you want to push me away. It's because you're scared.'

She took a small step towards him, trying to find the words that would make him see that she would never hurt him.

'But you don't need to be. Not any more. Not with me. You can trust me.' She took a deep breath. 'That's what I was going to tell you—'

His face looked glittering and hard and impenetrable, like a diamond. 'What were you going to tell me?'

For a split second she felt as though she were standing on a window ledge. Fear, thicker and blacker than smoke, filled her lungs and then, shaking her head, she gave a small, strangled laugh.

'I was going to tell you that I love you.'

He stared at her, the expression on his face so still and blank that she thought he hadn't understood her.

And then he said slowly, 'Then it's probably a good thing that you found those plans now. Keep your love, *cara*, for someone who wants it.'

He watched her face, saw the flash of pain and knew that he wasn't being fair or kind. But that simply seemed to wind him up more tightly, and he couldn't stop the rush of anger rising inside him.

She might trust him, but he sure as hell didn't trust *her*—or anyone else for that matter. And he would certainly never trust anyone enough to love them.

It wasn't his fault.

It was just how it had to be.

And he'd been fair. He hadn't promised what he couldn't give. Nor had he lied about what he wanted. And he didn't want her love. Hell, he'd never even asked for it. Yet now she was trying to make him feel guilty about that!

'I didn't intend for any of this to happen,' he said roughly. 'You and I. Us.'

Her head jerked up. 'I thought there *was* no "us",' she said, unable to hide her bitterness. 'There's not even really a me, is there? You're the only one that matters—aren't you, Massimo?'

She watched him, saw his face close and harden.

'So when were you going to make yourself homeless?'

His eyes met hers. 'I don't know. I didn't think that far ahead.'

In part it was true. Since he'd arrived at the *palazzo* his life had been turned upside down. Normally his days were micromanaged to the last minute. Now, though, he seemed to have lost the ability to think beyond the immediate present.

He frowned. It was also true that he'd deliberately avoided even thinking about the development—let alone broaching it with Flora. But so what if he had? It was nothing to do with her. And if she didn't like that fact, that was her problem. She shouldn't have tried to make things personal.

Flora felt something shudder through her bones. He was

lying. For weeks now she'd seen him at work. He was on top of everything. No detail escaped his eye. With a stab of misery she remembered her dress fitting. No, he *knew*: he knew exactly when he'd been going to tell her.

And suddenly so did she. It would have been when he took her back to Rome in a couple of weeks.

Blood was roaring inside her head and shakily she reached out to grip the back of a chair.

'You *used* me!' She was so angry that she was glad there was a table between them. 'Of all the low things you've done, this is the absolute—'

'What are you talking about?'

Her eyes met his. How could she have been so gullible? A man like Massimo could have sex every hour on the hour with a different woman if he wanted. Yet not once had she ever questioned his attraction to her. She clenched her teeth. But then she didn't have his low morals; she couldn't just use anything or anyone to get what she wanted.

'I thought you wanted this house. And then I thought you wanted sex. But this was never about the *palazzo*. And it wasn't about the sex either. It was always just about the *deal*. Building that resort.' She gestured towards the plans in disgust.

For a moment she thought of how it could have been. Of what it might have been like to love Massimo and be loved by him. And suddenly she was fighting tears. Gritting her teeth, she breathed in sharply. It was *not* the end. It was the beginning. For now she knew that love was no longer something to be feared or shunned. And one day she would give her heart to someone who would treat it like the priceless gift it was.

She lifted her face and stared at him. What was she doing? Why was she having this pointless, excruciating conversation? There was nothing more to be said. And nothing more to do here.

With shock, she realised that she didn't need to keep hiding in Sardinia. Massimo Sforza had just trampled on her heart. If she could survive that then she could face her father and her brother. It was time to go home. To England. To her family.

She held his gaze for a moment and then, turning, walked swiftly out of the room.

Massimo stared after her. Not a muscle had moved on his face but inside he felt something like panic stir inside him. Never had a conversation spiralled so badly out of his control. Every word he'd spoken had simply seemed to make things worse.

But it wasn't his fault, he thought angrily. Last night had unsettled him—for obvious reasons. And she knew that.

So why couldn't she just have backed off? Instead of grilling him about matters that didn't even concern her? And telling him she loved him?

What the hell did she expect him to do with *that* piece of information?

It was her choice to feel like that. She could have kept it to herself. But instead she'd had to go and tell him. But why? Did she think he was going to fall down on bended knee and propose to her? Well, he wasn't. He wasn't the right man for her. And she shouldn't have put him in the position of having to say so. Nor should she have got upset at hearing the truth. It was far better *for both of them* that he made it clear right now that their relationship was always going to be purely sexual.

He gritted his teeth. Why should he have to remind her of that, anyway? Just because he'd told her about his past it didn't mean he owed her anything.

His stomach tightened painfully.

Except that he did.

Remembering the warmth and worry on her face as she'd listened to him talking about his father and Alida, he felt his anger slide away. She had helped him face up to his childhood. Even though he'd lashed out at her she'd stood her ground, pushing back when he pushed her away. Until finally she'd broken through the layers of protection he'd put up between himself and the world and freed him from the burden of his past.

He breathed out unsteadily.

Was he really not going to go after her?

Heart racing, he walked quickly out of the kitchen and ran up the stairs two at a time. Her bedroom was empty. His too. Mouth drying, he stepped back into her room. At first glance it looked unchanged. Her clothes were still in the wardrobe. A book she was struggling to finish lay spine-up on her bedside table.

Turning sharply, he felt a rush of pain. Her rucksack was no longer hanging on the back of the door. Nor was the folder containing her thesis on the dressing table. Blood was pounding in his ears. Feeling light-headed, he stumbled into the bathroom intending to splash his face with cold water—and then he saw it. Her dress. The blue silk lay draped over a chair, like the discarded skin of some mythical creature. And resting on top of it, scribbled on the bottom of her tenancy agreement, was a note.

Congratulations. You win. You got what you wanted. You closed the deal.

CHAPTER TEN

SLUMPING BACK IN his seat, Massimo stared at the men and women sitting around the boardroom table and frowned. All of them were white-faced and trembling. Some of the women seemed close to tears.

He'd lost his temper. It had been spectacular, brutal and unfair. But he didn't feel fair.

He felt angry.

And spread out on the table in front of him was the reason why.

The plans for the Sardinia resort. Nine weeks ago they'd been a glittering prize, waiting to be held aloft at the end of a challenging, arduous race. Now, though, the mere sight of them made him want to kick the table across the room.

Abruptly, he stood up and walked towards the floor-to-ceiling glass windows that ran the length of one wall, his eyes tracking the small clouds drifting slowly above the humming centre of Rome.

Where were they going? At some point would she look up and see them too?

At the thought of Flora, he felt his stomach clench painfully. And suddenly he wanted to be alone—alone with his anger and frustration.

'There's a lot to think about,' he said tersely, not bothering to turn round. 'Let's take the weekend and reschedule for Monday.'

The meeting was over.

Behind him, the sound of shuffling feet and papers told him that his staff were leaving. After a few moments he heard the door to the boardroom close with a soft click.

Sighing heavily, he added remorse to the list of feelings churning around inside his chest. His behaviour hadn't just been unreasonable; it had been completely incomprehensible as far as his staff were concerned. The Sardinian development was ready and waiting for the contractors to move in. Work on-site could have started today or yesterday or even a week ago.

So why the delay?

Remembering his fury when someone had asked him that very question, he gritted his teeth.

He knew the answer, of course. That was why he'd lost his temper. But what else could he have done? He certainly couldn't tell them the truth.

But now, alone, with no one to answer to except himself, his anger seeped away, leaving an aching hole in the pit of his stomach. The truth was there was no good reason to wait. There wasn't even a bad one. There was nothing except a feeling—a sense that once the *palazzo* was demolished what had happened between him and Flora would finally and irretrievably be over.

He felt a sudden, painful sting of frustration and, turning, he began to pace the room.

What was he thinking?

It couldn't be over because it had never actually started. Aside from the cohabiting, their affair had been exactly the same as every other he'd had. Probably the only reason he was even still thinking about her at all was because she'd stormed out on him.

His mouth twisted as he remembered how he'd sat and waited for her in the kitchen—hoping, believing that she would change her mind and come back. How finally, after several hours of increasing anger and frustration and despair, he'd got in his car and driven round the island looking for her. He hadn't found her. And instead of having the chance to throw her accusations back in her face he'd been left alone to brood in an empty house, where every single room was filled with reminders of her absence.

Was it any wonder he couldn't just forget her?

He was still mulling over that thought when there was a soft tap on the boardroom door.

'What is it?' he said irritably.

The door opened slowly and a hand slid through, waving a red paisley handkerchief.

Massimo frowned. 'Is this some kind of mime show or are you stripping? Because, as stripteases go, I have to say it's not doing that much for me.'

He watched as Giorgio stuck his head round the door. 'It should really be white.'

Massimo smiled reluctantly. 'So why are you surrendering?'

Stepping into the room, the lawyer glanced at him nervously. 'I've got a family so I need to stay alive!' He shot his boss a furtive look. 'Apparently it was a bit of bloodbath at the board meeting.'

Massimo sighed. 'Is that what they're saying?'

Giorgio shook his head. 'They're not saying anything! But given that it looks a bit *28 Days Later* out there, I just took an educated guess.'

There was a long, strained silence, and then abruptly Massimo yanked the nearest chair away from the table and sat down heavily. 'I was a little short,' he admitted finally. 'But I just need a bit more time...'

His words trailed off and, leaning back in the chair, he rubbed his hand slowly over the top of his neck. A headache was forming, and more than anything he just wanted to lie down in a dark room and go to sleep. Except that wouldn't actually happen. Since arriving back in Rome he'd barely managed more than an hour or two a night on the sofa. He'd lost his appetite too—which probably wasn't helping the headaches that punctuated his days and nights with monotonous regularity.

As though reading his mind, Giorgio cleared his throat and, pulling up a chair beside him, he said quietly, 'You look exhausted. Why not have an early night? Use the weekend to recharge. Get some focus.'

Massimo stared up at the ceiling. That was the other problem. He couldn't focus on *anything*. Certainly not work. He'd tried upping his exercise regime, to no effect. And his standard go-to for clearing his brain—a night or three with a beautiful, eager woman—held no appeal for him whatsoever. Not since Sardinia. Not since Flora.

The lawyer frowned. 'I mean it. Go home!'

Glancing at Giorgio, Massimo gave him a small, tight smile. 'That's a good idea—'

And it was—in theory.

Only the truth was he didn't have a home.

He owned properties: he'd added another three to his portfolio only last week. But none of them was a home, and the thought of spending a long weekend sitting alone in one of his hotel suites made a spasm of disproportionate misery squeeze his stomach tightly.

'But I really should get up to speed with everything,' he said slowly.

Nodding, Giorgio pulled out his phone and swiped rapidly across the screen. 'In that case there's a dinner tonight with the Minister of Finance. A lot of foreign investors are going to be there—including that Chinese consortium we worked with last year.' The lawyer hesitated, his face carefully expressionless. 'And we have a meeting in about an hour to discuss first-stage publicity for the Sardinia development.'

There was a sudden stillness in the room.

Massimo felt his skin tighten. The muscles in his back were rigid and it hurt to breathe. Did every damn conversation he had have to come back to Sardinia? He didn't even want to think about the development, let alone spend an afternoon discussing it in detail.

Frowning, he pressed his fingers against his forehead, where a new ache was starting to form. 'I thought we'd agreed to push everything back on that?' he muttered.

Giorgio shrugged. 'We did. But there's no harm in talking.'

Massimo shivered. 'Maybe I will take the afternoon off after all. I don't feel great. Is there such a thing as Sardinian flu?' he joked weakly.

There was a sudden shifting silence, and the lawyer cleared his throat. 'There could be.' He frowned, as though considering the possibility. 'What are your symptoms?'

Massimo hesitated for a moment and then shrugged. 'Nothing specific. I can't sleep. My appetite's shot. I've got no concentration.'

Irritably, he glanced around the empty boardroom. What kind of illness made you snap at your staff until they cried? Or made you so distracted they had to repeat everything they said to you?

Something was nagging at him—something obvious, yet nameless, and just out of reach.

Feeling Giorgio's gaze, he shifted in his seat. 'Ever since I got back to Rome I haven't felt myself. Joking aside, do you think I *might* have picked something up in Sardinia?'

'Maybe,' Giorgio said quietly. 'Although perhaps it's not what you picked up but what you left behind.'

'I didn't leave anything behind...' he began confusedly. 'The *palazzo* was empty—'

The air seemed to swell, as though it were holding back a secret, and Massimo felt his heart start to pound.

'The house was empty...' he said again.

'But *she's* still there somewhere, isn't she? Miss Golding, I mean?' Giorgio prompted gently. 'She won't have left the island. It's her home.'

And suddenly Massimo knew what was wrong with him.

He knew why he couldn't sleep or eat.

Or concentrate on anything for more than a few minutes.

And he knew why he didn't want to knock down the *palazzo*.

He was in love with Flora.

And the *palazzo* wasn't just some random building. It had been their home, somewhere he'd felt excited, happy, relaxed and safe. Safe enough to face his past. Only he couldn't have done it without Flora—with her, he had become whole.

Looking down at his lap, he saw to his surprise that his hands were shaking. Lifting his head, he found Giorgio watching him, his broad face creased with kindness.

'How did you know I was in love?' His face twisted. 'I mean, when...?'

The lawyer smiled. 'I saw the two of you together—' he cleared his throat '—in the garden, remember?'

Their eyes met, and Massimo breathed out. 'Oh, yes,' he said slowly. 'I forgot you were there.'

Giorgio laughed. 'That's when I knew. You only had eyes for each other.'

Massimo stared at him dazedly. Had Giorgio really been there that day? He had no memory of him at all. Or of the rest of the day, for that matter. All he could picture was Flora, singing softly to herself, her near naked body still damp from the pond.

'I don't understand,' he said shakily. 'I *can't* be in love. I don't know *how* to love.'

Patting him on the shoulder, Giorgio smiled ruefully. 'That's what everyone says. I certainly did when I fell in love with Anna. I actually broke up with her because it scared me so much.' He started to laugh. 'Then I saw her one evening, all dressed up to go out, and I walked into a door. That's what it took to knock it into my thick head.' He grinned. 'Then all I had to do was find Anna and tell her how I felt—'

Lowering his head into hands, Massimo groaned.

'I don't know where she is,' he said slowly. He looked up at Giorgio, his expression strained. 'We had a row and she stormed out.'

'We can find her,' the lawyer said firmly. 'It won't be that hard. She doesn't exactly blend in, does she?'

Massimo shook his head. 'It won't make any difference. After the way I treated her she's not going to want anything to do with me.'

Giorgio stood up. 'Then you *make* her want to,' he said, slapping Massimo around the shoulders.

'If you can't then you don't deserve her. And you're not the man who persuaded me to join his start-up business for less than half the salary I was getting from my previous job.'

Massimo's eyes gleamed. 'I was worth it, though, wasn't I?'

'Don't tell *me* that. Tell *her*!'

Gritting his teeth, he felt a rush of determination—hot

and strong-flowing, like blood. He'd been a fool. Never in all his business dealings had he been so blind, so utterly clueless. All the signs that he loved Flora were there. He'd looked forward to spending time with her. Not just having sex but talking and teasing, being teased. Listening to her talk about her mother's death, he had *cared* that she was hurting. More than cared: he'd wanted to take away her pain.

But it had never occurred to him that he was falling in love with her.

He hadn't even realised it was love he was feeling.

All he'd sensed was that for the first time since his childhood he'd felt vulnerable. Caring, loving, needing were all reminders of a past that had left deep and painful scars. So when he'd started to care about Flora, he'd got scared. Scared that a woman might once again have power over him—power over how he should feel, power to hurt him. And he'd panicked. So terrified by what he was feeling that he'd pushed her away, his fear blinding him to her kindness and her courage. Even to her love.

He breathed out slowly. That fear felt like nothing now. Not beside the realisation that he'd made the biggest mistake of his life: that having rejected her, he needed Flora and her love in order to live.

Pushing back the chair, he straightened his shoulders and stood up. Grabbing Giorgio's hand, he shook it firmly. 'You're a good man, Giorgio. A good friend too. I'm going to take your advice, so I won't be joining you for dinner.'

The lawyer frowned, then nodded. He was watching his boss intently. 'Do you want me to reschedule a meeting with the Chinese next week?'

Massimo glanced around the boardroom. It represented his life's work. His legacy. But it wasn't enough. His eyes

flared, but his face was calm and certain. 'That depends...
On when we get back.'

Giorgio raised an eyebrow.

Massimo grinned. 'I'm going to Sardinia to find her,
Giorgio. And when I do I'm going to prove to her that I
love her. However long that takes.'

Flora flopped back against the faded sofa cushions and
stared miserably out of the window at the rain-sodden garden. After Sardinia, England felt incredibly cold and grey
and wet. And, as if the weather outside wasn't bad enough,
inside the house it was distinctly stormy too.

She frowned. It was her own fault. Turning up on her
dad's doorstep, having clearly been howling her head off,
and then trying to pretend nothing was wrong had been
asking for trouble.

Sighing, she got up from the sofa, dragged on a pair
of boots and a coat and stomped out the front door. The
trouble was that her father had never really come to terms
with her being an adult. Obviously he knew how old she
was, but he just couldn't accept that she was capable of
making her own decisions.

And now she'd done the worst thing possible. She'd
proved him right.

Her dad had been horrified to see her so upset and then,
having recovered his equilibrium, he'd immediately started
to take charge of her life. Within twenty minutes he'd got
hold of a friend who ran a horticultural business and ar-
ranged an interview for Flora. Next he'd cajoled her into
choosing new wallpaper and curtains for her bedroom.

Still reeling from the shock and pain of Massimo's rejection, she hadn't had the strength to argue. It had been
easier just to acquiesce to his wishes. But then Freddie had

come home yesterday, and she'd remembered exactly why she'd fled to Sardinia in the first place.

It was hard enough trying to stand up to her father, but against her dad and Freddie united it was impossible.

It had stopped raining now, and the sun was trying to push its way through the drifting clouds. In the park, two small children were playing under the watchful eye of their father. Staring at them, Flora felt a shiver of despair. Being protective was perfectly natural, but Freddie and her dad were so overprotective it was stifling.

At least she'd managed to stop Freddie from flying out to Sardinia. Remembering her brother's fury when finally she'd given him a severely edited version of the truth, Flora winced. He'd actually been far angrier with himself than with Flora, but that had actually made her feel worse. Him thinking that she couldn't cope... As if she was useless or helpless or both.

The park was empty now and, glancing at her watch, she saw that it was nearly lunchtime. Reluctantly, she began walking home. After leaving Sardinia, it had taken her a few days to realise when she needed to eat. At first she'd confused the near permanent ache inside in her chest with hunger, until finally it had occurred to her that it had nothing to do with food. And everything to do with Massimo.

Unbidden, hot, swift tears rose in her throat. She missed him so much. And instead of diminishing day by day the pain in her heart seemed to be growing stronger—driven in part by the knowledge that perhaps, had she channelled that last devastating conversation differently, she might not even be back in England. But it had been so hard and he'd been so unapproachable, so brutal.

She felt a sudden flash of anger. It wouldn't have mattered what she'd said or how she'd said it. The outcome would have been the same. Massimo didn't love her. She wasn't even sure he knew how to love.

Glancing up, she saw that she was back at her dad's house and, with a sigh, she pushed open the back door.

'Where have you been?'

It was Freddie. His face was creased with exasperation.

'I went for a walk.'

His eyes narrowed. 'And you didn't think to tell Dad?' Punching buttons on his phone, he shook his head. 'I need to tell him you're back. He went out looking for you in the car!' He stopped. 'Yes…No…She's here…No. She's fine. I'll see you in a minute.'

Feeling like a child who'd been caught with her hand in the biscuit tin, Flora hung up her coat shakily. 'I was only gone a few minutes, Freddie.'

Her brother stared at her, his face flushed, his grey eyes dark like storm clouds. 'You were gone for nearly an *hour*, Flora.'

Her face grew still. He was right. She'd looked at her watch and seen the time for herself. Only it hadn't registered. Nothing really registered at the moment.

Freddie shook his head. 'You are *so* selfish sometimes. Do you have *any* idea how worried Dad's been about you?'

'I didn't—' she began.

But Freddie interrupted her. 'I'm not talking about now. I'm talking about all the time you were away. All that time—day and night—he was waiting for a phone call to say you'd been hurt or worse. It was bad enough that you ran away like that—'

Flora swallowed. It wasn't fair of Freddie to try and make her feel guilty about what she'd done. She *had* run away—but only because if she'd told them she wanted to go they would have talked her out it.

Her brother stared at her irritably. 'And then when something *does* happen you don't even tell us.'

'There was no point,' Flora said quickly. 'I was coming home. And nothing really happened.'

'He *hurt* you. How can you say that's nothing?'

'I'm not.' She glowered at him. Her temper felt thin and worn about the edges. 'He *did* hurt me, but being hurt is part of life, Freddie. I can't stay in my bedroom all my life, playing make-believe!'

Her brother scowled at her. 'I should never have let you go over there. And I certainly shouldn't have let you stay on living there when that snake Sforza moved in.'

Flora felt a flash of anger. 'It wasn't up to you, Freddie. I'm a grown-up—'

The door opened behind her and, seeing the anxiety and worry on her dad's face, she felt her anger give way to guilt.

'Flora, darling! I was so worried about you—'

Her father pulled her into his arms and she felt a rush of love mingled with irritation as she felt his racing heartbeat. She pulled away. 'I'm fine, Dad. I just needed to get out of the house. I took a coat and everything.' She smiled weakly.

'Everything except your phone,' Freddie snapped.

'Why would I need my phone? I was walking round the village.' She glared at him. 'The village we grew up in. Look, I know you both worry about me, but I'm not a child. I went to university. I've had jobs. And I've lived in a foreign country. On my own.'

Freddie snorted. 'And look how *that* turned out!'

Something inside her seemed to tear apart.

Turning, she faced her brother, her teeth pressing hard against each another. 'It turned out fine. I don't know what you think happened out there, but I left on *my* terms. And I'm going back on my terms too.'

There was a short, frayed silence, and then her father said slowly, 'Flora! I don't understand. You can't seriously be thinking about going back?'

'She's not,' said Freddie, staring at his sister with naked frustration. 'She's going to stay here, where we can keep an eye on her.'

Their eyes met. Normally this was the moment when she'd back down. Even before he'd become a lawyer she hadn't been able to fight the way her brother did. But since he'd become a barrister he was just in a different league when it came to questioning and confrontation.

'It's for your own good, Flora. It's not like there aren't orchids in England. You can easily finish your dissertation here.'

She nodded dumbly and, sensing her capitulation, he smiled. 'It's the right thing to do, Flossie.' He was calming down, his voice losing that implacable force. 'Dad and I— We're not trying to be mean. We just don't want to see you get hurt again. And I promise you it's not about stopping you from doing what you want to do. If you could think of one good reason to go back to that *palazzo* then we wouldn't stand in your way. But you can't, can you?'

One good reason.

Flora stared at him in silence. She *could* think of one very good reason to go back to Sardinia. In fact, it wasn't just a good reason, it was the best reason in the world: *love*.

Lifting her chin, she nodded slowly. 'Yes. I can. And that's why I'm going back, Freddie.' She turned to her father. 'I know you miss Mum. I do too. And what happened to her was awful. But it happened *here*, because bad things happen everywhere.'

Reaching out, she took her father's hand and then, after a moment's hesitation, she took Freddie's too.

'I know you love me, and I love you both—only you can't keep me safe and sound.' She bit her lip. 'But you *can* trust me to look after myself. I know it's hard, and I know I haven't always given you reason to believe me, but—' she squeezed both their hands tightly '—I *need* to do this,' she said firmly. 'So, will you please let me go back?'

Slowly her father nodded, and then finally Freddie nodded too.

'But you have to promise that you'll call if you need us.'

She smiled weakly. 'I'll always need both of you. But right now someone else needs me more.'

The sun was reaching its peak in the sky, high above the *palazzo*. Massimo stared moodily across the *terrazza*. It was too hot to be inland and he'd half considered taking the yacht out. But he couldn't bring himself to leave the house—not even for an afternoon.

He wanted to be there, just in case Flora came back. Picking up his glass of wine, he drank slowly and deliberately.

Not that there was any reason to think that she *was* coming back. In all honesty there was no reason to think that he would ever see her again.

It had been nearly eight days since he'd told Giorgio that he was going to find Flora. Eight days of false leads and dashed hopes. It had sounded so promising at first. He'd tracked her to Cagliari, and then over to England. But since then there had been no trace of her. She'd simply disappeared.

Lifting his gaze, he watched a jewel-bright dragonfly hover lazily above the fountain. He had been so sure he would find her. So sure he'd be able to win her back.

But now he saw that his certainty had been based solely on optimism. Not on statistical probability. After all, on a planet of six billion people, what were the odds of him finding her?

Truthfully, she could be anywhere.

And after the way he'd treated her the chances of her ever stepping through those kitchen doors again were minimal. Less than zero, in fact.

He poured another glass of wine. This was definitely the one place on earth she'd never want to set eyes on again. *Hell!* He shouldn't even *be* here. Only he couldn't seem to leave.

He glanced round the garden, his skin tightening. Or rather he didn't *want* to leave. Here, he could let his imagination drift. He could almost see her disappearing under an archway at the end of the garden, hear her laughter from inside the kitchen.

Sitting up straighter, he shook his head. If he was chasing shadows…phantoms, it must be time to move. Standing up unsteadily, he picked the bottle off the table and began to walk slowly across the lawn. Beneath his bare feet the grass felt hot and parched, and he could feel the wine working its way through his blood.

Softly he began to hum under his breath. He couldn't quite place the tune, but he knew he remembered it from somewhere.

And then he heard it.

Someone was singing—singing the words to the song he was humming.

His heart started to pound. It was a woman's voice. Soft, husky, familiar.

Squinting up into the sun, he let the alcohol and the heat mingle with his memories. It wasn't her. He knew that, of course. It was just his imagination. But he didn't care.

Slowly, as though mesmerised, he followed the voice across the lawn. But as he stepped through the arch that led into the water garden the singing stopped. Hesitating, he stared through the foliage, his heart pounding painfully in his chest, hope twitching in every muscle.

But of course she wasn't there.

For a moment he stood, swaying slightly, and then carefully he walked towards the large rectangular ornamental pond that gave the garden its name. The surface was dotted with water lilies, their waxy white petals splaying up towards the sun, and he stared at them in fascination. And then suddenly he jerked backwards, grabbing the arm of a beautiful marble statue to keep his balance, as a naked woman broke the surface of the water, rising up slowly.

She had her back to him.

But he would know the curve of that spine anywhere—even in the darkness. It was Flora.

His head was spinning; his breath was hot and dry in his throat.

It couldn't be her.

He must be imagining it. Or it was some kind of optical illusion. Any moment now the sun would go behind a cloud and she would disappear for ever.

Holding his breath, he watched as with effortless grace she pulled herself onto one of the marble slabs edging the pond, smoothing her hair back over the contours of her head.

He took a deep breath. It didn't matter that she wasn't real. He was happy just to stand there and watch her. He frowned. Maybe he could even get a little closer.

Letting go of the statue's arm, he put the bottle down on the ground and stepped forward just as she turned around.

She stopped, one foot slightly raised like a deer at the edge of a meadow. And then slowly she frowned and folded her arms. 'I know you're the landlord, but tenants have rights too. Including privacy while bathing. It's in my contract.'

Massimo gazed at her dazedly. 'Flora?'

She stared at him impatiently. 'Is that the best you can do? Pretend you don't know who I am?'

'I— No— I *do* know who you are. Of *course*. I thought you were...' He hesitated. 'It doesn't matter.'

He watched, transfixed, as she picked her way across the stones and came towards him, his eyes following the droplets of water trickling down over her naked breasts and stomach.

She was real. What was more, she was *there*, standing in front of him.

'What are you doing here?' he murmured.

She glowered at him. 'I live here, remember? This is my home.'

His eyes met hers and she almost flinched. She'd forgotten how it felt to be the object of that gaze. How tight and hot and restless it made her feel.

But she hadn't come back for that gaze.

This time it wasn't enough.

This time she wanted more.

But he had to want it too.

'Never mind about me,' she said hoarsely. 'What about you?' She glanced slowly round the garden. 'I thought you'd be long gone and all this razed to the ground.'

They stared at one another in silence.

Finally, he shrugged. 'Things have changed.'

He watched her lip curl, his heart beating in his throat. How had he ever imagined she was a figment of his imagination? She was so clear and vital. Beside her everything else seemed smudged and dull and imprecise.

'What things?' she snapped.

He smiled then, that same sweet smile that made her feel hot and dizzy and restless, and suddenly she felt more naked than when she'd climbed out of the pond.

Abruptly, she turned and picked up a faded blue shirt. Tugging it over her head, she breathed out slowly, grateful for a chance to break free of that dark, disturbing gaze. Being so close to Massimo was playing havoc with her body temperature. But she wasn't going to give in to the heat rising inside of her.

He shrugged, his gaze never leaving her face.

'It's complicated but in all probability the resort won't happen, *cara*.'

She stared at him suspiciously. 'Have you got that in writing?'

He laughed out loud. 'You know, you sound exactly like your brother. Thankfully, you don't *look* like him.'

Her face twisted. 'How do you know what my brother looks like?'

The air around them twitched. Her heart gave a jolt as he stepped towards her, his face tightening.

'I met him. Your father too.'

Suddenly she could hardly breathe. 'When?' she said woodenly. 'Where?'

'A couple of days ago. In England. You have the same colour eyes.' Gently, he reached out and touched her cheek, and her heart began to pound so loudly she thought her chest would burst.

'Why were you there?' she said hoarsely.

His eyes were soft and blue and loving. 'Why do you think?'

She shook her head. 'No. You *say* it, Massimo. But only if you mean it.'

He stepped closer...so close that she could feel the heat of his skin through his shirt.

'I went to find you so I could tell you that I love you. And that I need you. Now. And tomorrow. And for ever.'

Her eyes filled with tears. He pulled her closer but she pushed hard against his chest. 'Why should I trust you? You *hurt* me.'

'I know. And I'm sorry. Sorrier than you'll ever know.'

Her heart quivered. Massimo was apologising. In some strange way she knew that was as big a step as his declaration of love.

But still she needed more. 'I told you I loved you and you told me to keep my love for someone who wanted it.'

'I *do* want it. I love you, *cara*.' His face was pale and taut, but his gaze was clear and unwavering. 'More than I ever believed I could love anyone. And it was you that made me believe. It was you who made me whole and strong. Strong enough to let the past go and fight for my future. Fight for what I want.'

'What about this place? You wanted that?'

He nodded. 'I did. But not any more. In fact, as of yesterday, I don't even own it.'

Seeing the confusion and fear in her eyes, he shook his head. 'Don't worry. The new owner wants it left just as it is.'

'How do you know?' she said shakily. He smiled.

'Because she told me she wouldn't let me turn it into some "ghastly boutique hotel for loud, sweaty, tourists"!' Flora gasped.

'What have you done?' she whispered.

'I've signed this place over to you—'

'But— Is that why you're here?' Her hands gripped the

front of his shirt. He shook his head, his eyes suddenly too bright.

'No. I came back to wait for you. And to do what I should have done when you told me you loved me.'

Reaching into his pocket, he pulled out a small square box and, opening it, he held it out to her. It was a beautiful diamond ring, edged with sapphires.

'I want you to be my wife, Flora. And I want this to be our home. Some of the time, anyway.'

Searching his face, Flora felt her heart contract. There was no anger or bitterness or doubt. He looked happy and utterly assured.

'Will you marry me?' he said softly, taking her hand in his.

She stared at the ring fiercely. For so long marriage had represented everything she feared most.

But now, looking into his unguarded face, she was no longer afraid to hope or to believe in love.

Smiling up at him, she nodded, and he slid the ring smoothly onto her finger. And then his mouth came down on hers and he kissed her with a passion that was hotter and fiercer than the Sardinian sun.

Finally, they broke apart. Looking up, she knew that the expression on his face exactly matched the way she was feeling and then, loosening his grip, he glanced down at her and frowned.

'Is that my shirt?'

She shrugged 'I might have found it in your wardrobe.'

She watched his eyes glitter with amusement, and something dark and warm that sent shivers of longing dancing down her spine.

'I think the word you're looking for, *cara*, is *stole*!'

Her insides quivered as with slow deliberation he slid his hand beneath the shirt.

'I found it. So now it's mine. Possession is nine-tenths of the law!'

Suddenly the intensity in his eyes matched the probing pressure of his touch.

'I wouldn't argue with that!'

She stared at him, her skin prickling. 'You wouldn't?'

He shook his head, his hand curling possessively around her hipbone. 'No. You see, I found you in my garden. Which is now your garden. That means I'm yours. And you're mine. *All* mine.'

'What about the other tenth?' she whispered.

He smiled that slow, sweet smile again and her pulse began to race as she felt the soft, probing progress of his fingers over her bare skin.

'I rounded it up to make things easier.'

And, lowering his mouth, he kissed her slowly and hungrily.

* * * * *

MILLS & BOON®
Hardback – February 2016

ROMANCE

Leonetti's Housekeeper Bride	Lynne Graham
The Surprise De Angelis Baby	Cathy Williams
Castelli's Virgin Widow	Caitlin Crews
The Consequence He Must Claim	Dani Collins
Helios Crowns His Mistress	Michelle Smart
Illicit Night with the Greek	Susanna Carr
The Sheikh's Pregnant Prisoner	Tara Pammi
A Deal Sealed by Passion	Louise Fuller
Saved by the CEO	Barbara Wallace
Pregnant with a Royal Baby!	Susan Meier
A Deal to Mend Their Marriage	Michelle Douglas
Swept into the Rich Man's World	Katrina Cudmore
His Shock Valentine's Proposal	Amy Ruttan
Craving Her Ex-Army Doc	Amy Ruttan
The Man She Could Never Forget	Meredith Webber
The Nurse Who Stole His Heart	Alison Roberts
Her Holiday Miracle	Joanna Neil
Discovering Dr Riley	Annie Claydon
His Forever Family	Sarah M. Anderson
How to Sleep with the Boss	Janice Maynard

MILLS & BOON®
Large Print – February 2016

ROMANCE

Claimed for Makarov's Baby	Sharon Kendrick
An Heir Fit for a King	Abby Green
The Wedding Night Debt	Cathy Williams
Seducing His Enemy's Daughter	Annie West
Reunited for the Billionaire's Legacy	Jennifer Hayward
Hidden in the Sheikh's Harem	Michelle Conder
Resisting the Sicilian Playboy	Amanda Cinelli
Soldier, Hero...Husband?	Cara Colter
Falling for Mr December	Kate Hardy
The Baby Who Saved Christmas	Alison Roberts
A Proposal Worth Millions	Sophie Pembroke

HISTORICAL

Christian Seaton: Duke of Danger	Carole Mortimer
The Soldier's Rebel Lover	Marguerite Kaye
Return of Scandal's Son	Janice Preston
The Forgotten Daughter	Lauri Robinson
No Conventional Miss	Eleanor Webster

MEDICAL

Hot Doc from Her Past	Tina Beckett
Surgeons, Rivals...Lovers	Amalie Berlin
Best Friend to Perfect Bride	Jennifer Taylor
Resisting Her Rebel Doc	Joanna Neil
A Baby to Bind Them	Susanne Hampton
Doctor...to Duchess?	Annie O'Neil

MILLS & BOON®
Hardback – March 2016

ROMANCE

The Italian's Ruthless Seduction	Miranda Lee
Awakened by Her Desert Captor	Abby Green
A Forbidden Temptation	Anne Mather
A Vow to Secure His Legacy	Annie West
Carrying the King's Pride	Jennifer Hayward
Bound to the Tuscan Billionaire	Susan Stephens
Required to Wear the Tycoon's Ring	Maggie Cox
The Secret That Shocked De Santis	Natalie Anderson
The Greek's Ready-Made Wife	Jennifer Faye
Crown Prince's Chosen Bride	Kandy Shepherd
Billionaire, Boss...Bridegroom?	Kate Hardy
Married for their Miracle Baby	Soraya Lane
The Socialite's Secret	Carol Marinelli
London's Most Eligible Doctor	Annie O'Neil
Saving Maddie's Baby	Marion Lennox
A Sheikh to Capture Her Heart	Meredith Webber
Breaking All Their Rules	Sue MacKay
One Life-Changing Night	Louisa Heaton
The CEO's Unexpected Child	Andrea Laurence
Snowbound with the Boss	Maureen Child

MILLS & BOON®
Large Print – March 2016

ROMANCE

A Christmas Vow of Seduction	Maisey Yates
Brazilian's Nine Months' Notice	Susan Stephens
The Sheikh's Christmas Conquest	Sharon Kendrick
Shackled to the Sheikh	Trish Morey
Unwrapping the Castelli Secret	Caitlin Crews
A Marriage Fit for a Sinner	Maya Blake
Larenzo's Christmas Baby	Kate Hewitt
His Lost-and-Found Bride	Scarlet Wilson
Housekeeper Under the Mistletoe	Cara Colter
Gift-Wrapped in Her Wedding Dress	Kandy Shepherd
The Prince's Christmas Vow	Jennifer Faye

HISTORICAL

His Housekeeper's Christmas Wish	Louise Allen
Temptation of a Governess	Sarah Mallory
The Demure Miss Manning	Amanda McCabe
Enticing Benedict Cole	Eliza Redgold
In the King's Service	Margaret Moore

MEDICAL

Falling at the Surgeon's Feet	Lucy Ryder
One Night in New York	Amy Ruttan
Daredevil, Doctor...Husband?	Alison Roberts
The Doctor She'd Never Forget	Annie Claydon
Reunited...in Paris!	Sue MacKay
French Fling to Forever	Karin Baine

MILLS & BOON®

Why shop at millsandboon.co.uk?

Each year, thousands of romance readers find their perfect read at millsandboon.co.uk. That's because we're passionate about bringing you the very best romantic fiction. Here are some of the advantages of shopping at www.millsandboon.co.uk:

* **Get new books first**—you'll be able to buy your favourite books one month before they hit the shops

* **Get exclusive discounts**—you'll also be able to buy our specially created monthly collections, with up to 50% off the RRP

* **Find your favourite authors**—latest news, interviews and new releases for all your favourite authors and series on our website, plus ideas for what to try next

* **Join in**—once you've bought your favourite books, don't forget to register with us to rate, review and join in the discussions

Visit **www.millsandboon.co.uk**
for all this and more today!